CON

SECRETS AND LIES BOOK 2

B J Alpha

CON

Secrets and Lies Series Book 2

Copyright © 2022 by B J Alpha

All rights reserved.

No part of this book may be reproduced or transmitted in either, electronic, paper hard copy, photocopying, recorded or any other form of reproduction without the written permission of the author. No part of this book either in part or whole may be reproduced into or stored in a retrieval system or distributed without the written permission of the author, except for the use of brief quotations in a book review.

This book is a work of fiction. Characters, names, places and incidents are products of the authors imagination or used fictitiously.

Any similarity to actual events, locations or persons living or dead is purely coincidental.

Without in any way limiting the author's exclusive rights under copyright, any use of this publication to "train" generative artificial intelligence (AI) technologies to generate text is expressly prohibited. The author reserves all rights to license uses of this work for generative AI training and development of machine learning language models. No audio files can be produced without the authors written consent beforehand.

Published by BJ Alpha

Edited by Dee Houpt

Cover Design by Katie Evans

Author Note

WARNING:

This book contains triggers. It contains sensitive and explicit storylines such as domestic abuse, mental health issues, sexual scenes with dubious consent and strong language recommended for readers aged eighteen and over.

Playlist

Remember - Becky Hill and David Guetta
Hold on (Acoustic) – Chord Overstreet
Broken – Jonah Kagen
Anyone - Justin Bieber
Save Me - Queen
Better Man (Acoustic) - Robbie Williams
Tell Me That You Love Me – James Smith
Bruises – Lewis Capaldi
Gravity – DJ Fresh
Mirrors - Justin Timberlake
Nobody Knows - The Lumineers

Dedication

Save Me For Myself
Dedicated to
TL Swan for giving me purpose
&

Bren Hawk for your support, understanding and friendship.

**For Con and to all of those who suffer with their
mental health.**

Save Me For Myself

Broken, empty, a shell of my former self,
Desperate, despondent, void of emotion,
Useless, worthless, unwanted,
Filled with self-loathing.

Shattered into a thousand pieces, fractured,
Destroyed beyond repair.
Save me from myself,
I need you to show me you care.

Build me, help me, love my broken self,
Hold me through this misery,
Take away my pain,
Support me to stand, to feel once again.

Save me, save me from myself.
Show me that you care,
Rebuild me, fill me with love and kindness,
Show me that you're there.

Hope, warmth, love,
Strength, compassion, happiness,
Cure me for myself,
Safe in your loving arms, comfort all around me.

Save me for myself.

Written by BJ Alpha

Prologue

Two Days Before ...

Con

As I sit around the table in my brother Bren's apartment, a familiar tingle of happiness washes over me. I don't feel this way often. I'm known as the jolly, happy-go-lucky brother, but truth be told, I feel anything but. I'm lost, an empty shell of my true self.

Sure, my brother Finn and I are and always have been thick as thieves. We've always enjoyed winding our older brothers up and excelling at our notorious playboy lifestyle to the fullest. I may exude happiness on the outside, but in reality, I am void of feelings. I wish I could feel a flicker of what I let others believe I'm experiencing.

But tonight? Tonight is one of those nights I genuinely look forward to. Once every two weeks or so, my brothers and I gather at one of our apartments and release our tensions with a good old game of poker. Throw in a few beers, junk food, and the banter we all get a kick out of, even Oscar—though he'd never admit it—and it's the best time.

I'd never tell my brothers this, but I'd actually rather play poker with these guys than have any random chick to fuck or suck my cock. How crazy is that?

Thriving on the excitement buzzing through me, I glance at my hand. Fucking luck is on my side tonight, but I refrain from grinning.

I scan the table, analyzing my competition.

Finn has a shit hand, it's a wonder his fucking toothpick hasn't given him splinters; he's chewing it that hard. Oscar has the same impassive expression. Does he look like that when he comes too? Cal has a smile tugging at his lips, making it obvious he's my competition and useless at hiding his hand. Bren throws his cards on the table in defeat. "I'm out! Shit hand again," he declares through gritted teeth.

Cal's eyes light up in amusement, his smug smile full of glee. "Full house!"

The cocky fucker thinks he's won. *Mmm, think again, sunshine.* "Royal Flush," I announce with a wink to piss off Cal.

Groans and swearing litter the table, and I smile to myself. This is turning out to be a damn good night, just what I fucking need.

Conversations go on around the table. I'm mildly amused and downright mortified about the things Cal is having to endure since his wife, Lily, had their daughter, Chloe.

Poor guy has a smoking-hot wife with a bulging fucking rack, yet he isn't allowed anywhere near them because her nipples are bleeding? Who knew that was a thing? I inwardly shudder. Thank fuck my little harem of women know better than to want more from me than a good fuck.

Don't get me wrong, a couple of them keep fucking hinting at a relationship, but that's not going to happen. Ever.

Oscar tells Cal how unhappy he is about the fact he swapped Lily's pill for fertility drugs. Of course, Cal puts him in line and tells him under no circumstances is she to find out. With all the fucking tension in the air, I throw another handful of peanuts in my mouth.

"So, the little charity event I attended Tuesday was interesting," Bren announces, and his eyebrows do a teasing wiggle.

"You get laid?" I ask. Let's face it, he's so intense he needs to get fucking laid.

"I got a hot piece of ass's cell number that I might call, but I was referring to seeing Con's ex-girlfriend looking all hot on stage and giving a speech." He whistles through his teeth, trying to wind me up. *Yeah, not biting, pal.* I roll my eyes internally.

I don't do girlfriends, therefore there's no ex. "Funny, I don't recall having an ex-girlfriend. Conquests, yes. Girlfriends, no." I give Bren a sly wink.

Here he goes … "That's funny. Could have sworn you once had a feisty little brunette hanging off your shoulder a few years ago." He shrugs.

My eyebrows pull together, thinking about who he's referring to. There's only one girl I ever openly showed any relationship behavior toward.

I glance at Cal and Finn, who both appear equally

confused. Then I glance at Oscar, who is looking just as unsure.

Bren smiles widely, way too happy with himself, and sits taller with a smug-as-fuck grin on his face. Yeah, he's confident, and he's got my attention. My heart is beating faster, and I sit up a little straighter, trying not to show him how much he's bothering me. "What the fuck are you talking about?" I all but snap.

"You mean *who* the fuck am I talking about?" Bren smirks, trying to be fucking clever. Not the time, motherfucker.

"Bren," Cal warns, "cut the fucking shit." Cal knows how I feel about her, and he's aware not to rile me up on the subject. Shit, he knows not to even broach the subject.

Bren sighs. "Okay, so I'm sitting at a boring-as-fuck charity event for Survivors of Domestic Abuse when who should walk on stage and give a speech? One of their representatives, which just so happens to be Will, and fuck, is she hot!" He exhales loudly for dramatic effect.

The room is silent. However, my heart is pounding in my chest so hard I'm surprised they can't hear it. My blood is rushing around my body, and at the mere mention of her name, I experience rage. I can't bear the thought of hearing her name. I close my eyes and try to pull myself together.

"Fuuuck," Finn drags out, breaking the silence.

Maybe I misheard? I open my eyes and glare at him. "Will. As in Will?"

He nods, meeting my eyes for emphasis on how sure he is. "Yeah, man, it was her. Honest to God. She had us all eating out the palm of her fucking hand. She looked stunning too." Bren laughs to himself. "Seriously, you'd have blown your fucking load at the table, Con." Is he for real right now?

"Will?" I ask again. You know, just to clarify.

I glance toward Cal, and he fidgets, like he knows I'm a fucking time bomb waiting to go off.

Bren chuckles. "Jesus, Con, if I thought you were going to go all fucking crazy, I wouldn't have bothered telling you." I have to breathe. He doesn't understand. He doesn't know what she means to me. If he did, he'd never joke around like this. I sit looking at the end of the table, lost in my own thoughts.

"She was at a Survivors of Domestic Abuse event as a key spokesperson?" Oscar asks in his serious tone. His voice breaks me out of my empty thoughts. And it suddenly registers. He saw Will, and she was speaking at a fucking domestic violence event? What the actual fuck?

I don't think. I erupt, and my chair hits the ground as I jump up.

Pointing at him, I state, "You went there Tuesday night, and it's now Friday! Why the hell did you wait until now to tell me this? And what is with the fucking domestic violence? What the fuck did she have to say? Who was she with?" Pacing behind the table, I can't gather my thoughts quick enough, and the dipshit hasn't answered one of my goddamn questions. My eyes bore into Bren, and his hands go through his hair, trying to rein his own temper in.

"Calm down, Con. Come on, it might not be what you're thinking," Cal says. He's trying to be the voice of reason, but it's fucking patronizing. I glare at him in annoyance, causing him to wince.

"Look, man, I really don't know much, and if I'm being brutally honest, I didn't hear anything she had to fucking say. I was a little taken aback by her being there on the stage. I mean, all fucking hot. The crowd liked her, though." Is he for real? Did he really just call the love of my life hot? The crowd fucking liked her? My eyes must appear crazy, because Finn's forehead creases and his Adam's apple bops slowly. He stares blankly at me, and his lips part but nothing comes out, causing his toothpick to fall from his mouth. He's completely at a loss for what to say, especially when I'm acting so out of character.

"Waste. Of. Fucking. Space!" Oscar snaps, breaking my train of thought.

"Well, how the fuck was I supposed to know he'd go all fucking crazy over her? Last I knew, they had a fucking breakup. Which was probably his fucking fault for being a dick to her as usual, and the poor girl must have come to her senses and got the fuck out of town!" I'm stunned. How the fuck can he know I screwed up? Am I that much of a fucking predictable loser? Is it that obvious I made the biggest fucking mistake of my life? He has no fucking idea. No idea what I went through, how I've fucking longed for her. How fucking dare he?

Rage bubbles to the surface, and I fly at him across the table; the snacks go everywhere, and beer bottles smash. Finn grabs my shoulders in a tight hold to restrain me. I've never wanted to hit my brother more than I do right now. Bren sits stoically still at the table in the same spot, in some sort of dazed shock.

Oscar jumps up from his chair and shouts, "Enough!" He exhales deeply. "I can access the event's guest list, find the guest speakers and representatives, and you can have her information by the morning, okay? No fucking harm done." He nods toward me, gritting his teeth.

I inwardly relax as Oscar's words sink in. I can have her details by tomorrow. Then I can find out what the hell has been going on in her life for her to be at a Survivors of Domestic Abuse event, and fuck, I could even see her again. Hope blossoms inside me.

Bren glances up from the table with a face etched with guilt. "Look, man, I'm sorry, okay? I didn't realize you still harbored feelings for her. If I'd have known …"

If he'd have known? If he'd have known, he'd never have fucking mentioned her. If he'd have known, he'd have kept her as far away from me as possible. Because what I did was unforgivable.

I don't let him finish. Turning on my heel, I march the fuck out the door. I need a fucking drink.

Chapter One

Con

I groan against the window of the SUV. Fuck, my head hurts.

What's that smell? Do I smell like fucking vomit? I pull my T-shirt to my nose, giving it a sniff. Yeah, vomit, beer, and cheap perfume.

Fuck, I'm such a disaster. I curl further into the passenger door. My head is pounding with each jerk of the car, and my eyes are stinging from the light.

After I don't know how fucking long, Oscar stops the car. I sit up and cast my eyes around. Where the hell has he brought me?

It's getting dark now, and we're parked on a street with nothing but a fancy-ass restaurant across the road. It's one of those posh-looking ones, the type with the arched canopy on the outside of the door, a small red carpet lining the entry way, and a doorman in a suit who waits to greet the customers.

I clear my throat. "Where the fuck are we?" I ask, glancing around trying to figure it out.

Oscar glares down at me from over his glasses, like I'm a piece of shit, and eyes me up and down. He shakes his head, as if ridding himself of all the terrible things he wants to say to me. He reaches into the back seat and pulls out a brown Manila folder, then drops it into my lap with a thud.

"What's this?" I ask.

Oscar sighs "Will's details, as promised." He nods at the folder, prompting me to open it.

I eye him with suspicion. "You promised me them on Saturday. It's now Sunday." Okay, so now I'm being a dick.

His eyes draw in and sharpen. "You're right, but you were, what shall I call it …? Otherwise engaged, weren't you? So, I let you continue your little pity party and collected your ass this afternoon before the party starts again this evening. Now, open the folder and let's deal with the next bit of unnecessary drama," he snaps, his face in a deadpan expression.

I stare at him in utter fucking shock. The guy is as emotionally suppressed as you can get. He's some sort of fucking sociopath. Is that what's wrong with him? Is that what a sociopath is? Someone who doesn't care about anything or anyone? If that's what one is, then yeah, Oscar is a fucking sociopath. I blink, trying to come back to fucking reality, but he snaps at me again before I can. "Connor, I don't have all fucking night! Are we dealing with this or not?"

His tone startles me, making me fucking jump and my heart hammer. "Fine. Fuck. You just don't give me fucking chance to think! Jesus, you're like some fucking sergeant major, barking fucking orders at me." His lips quirk into a sly smile. Yeah, that's Oscar's version of a fucking smile, weird prick.

I take a deep breath and open the folder; a photograph falls out.

I turn it around to scrutinize the picture. My fingers shake as I scan it; there's half a dozen people in the photo, but I see only one. Will. She's smiling among the group. It's the charity night, and the event banner is in the background. She's clearly with other representatives. They all seem professionally dressed, but Will stands out because she looks both professional and glamorous. She's the youngest in the picture and wearing a short red fitted dress and red high heels, so unlike the tomboy I remember. Sure, she would occasionally wear a dress or skirt around me, and she's always looked hot, but this?

This is another level of hotness; I can see why Bren was so mesmerized. Her long brunette hair is curled and draped over one shoulder, and her hazel eyes seem like they're glaring deep into my soul. Her plump fucking lips are red to match her dress. Fuck, those lips would be so fucking good wrapped around my cock again. As if on cue, my fucking cock starts to throb. I gulp and avert my gaze, feeling guilty I'm getting a hard-on sitting next to my brother while looking at a photo of a fully dressed woman. How fucking desperate. I hang my head in shame and scrub a hand through my hair.

I clear my throat. "That's her."

"It is," Oscar replies. His voice has a touch of sympathy in it as he bows his head in agreement.

My hands shake slightly as I move onto the next page. Surely, it's the hangover having this effect on me.

The next page holds some details I read aloud. "Ms.

Willow Chambers, age twenty-two years." I scoff at her name; Willow? She fucking hated being called Willow. Her full name she hated even more, Willowmena. Who the fuck names their kid that? Apparently, her mom wanted Willow, and her dad wanted Mena, a family name from her ancestors in Eastern Europe.

"She's divorced," he explains, breaking me away from my thoughts.

I study Oscar, then glance back at the sheet. It says Ms. "She married someone?" My heart beats rapidly against my chest, and anger swells inside me. She married someone who wasn't me.

Nodding, Oscar points out the next paragraph. "Married for two and a half years, hence the Ms. and the Chambers surname. She's now divorced, recently actually. She goes by the beginning of her first name now, Willow."

I nod, but for some reason, I'm ticked fucking off. She's been married and then divorced in what? Less than five years?

I read aloud again. "Jack Chambers, thirty-five, police officer for New Haven. A fucking pig! She married a fucking pig? What the hell was she thinking?" I erupt. My temple throbs, and the veins in my forehead pulsate. How could she do this to me?

Oscar's lips draw into a smirk. "I'd say she was thinking very well, or not so good at all. Depends on her story, I guess." He shrugs.

I spin and face him. "What the fuck are you talking about? Why do you always talk in such fucking riddles, Oscar? It takes us all forever to catch the fuck up with you!"

His lip curls up at the side of his mouth. "Well, if I

was trying to get away from domestic violence, a great idea would be to marry a police officer. Would it not?"

I let his comment sink in and think about it for a minute. He's right; he's always the logical one, and he's always thought of an answer before any of us can even process the question. "What if this guy, the pig, is the abuser?" I quiz.

Oscar shakes his head. "Doubt it. We're currently sitting outside a restaurant where Will is going to be attending a meal with the other representatives and her ex, Jack, to celebrate the success of the charity night."

My heart pounds, and my breathing turns erratic. He's fucking amazing. "She's going to be here tonight? How can you be sure?" I lick my lips, my throat suddenly dry with anticipation.

"Hacked her work emails." He shrugs again as though it's nothing.

I continue to flick through other parts of the file. It's mainly the usual things: birth certificate, bank statements, and so on. There's her work address and Jackass's work address. Information on their daily routines. There are two addresses on the file. One listed as Will's, 428 Elm Tree Grove, New Haven, Connecticut, and a different one for Jack. It looks like he got the apartment in the divorce and Will got the house.

"I didn't do a detailed search on them both. To be honest, I became a little stuck in certain areas. I'm assuming Jack knows people that help to keep information hidden. They've done a decent enough job that I'd need a little longer than twenty-four hours to extract it."

I peer at Oscar, confused by what he means.

He points to the file. "There's no bank information, just a standard statement that doesn't give Jack's earnings. There are no other bank account numbers other than the statement there, no hospital records, and Jack's profession is listed as a police officer. I imagine he's a little further up the chain than that, given he owns two properties and three vehicles. My guess is he's an FBI agent. Will's employment information is on there, but no details about any past employers and no salary. I mean, she could be a volunteer, but I'm guessing she earns something for her to run her own household."

I muse over Oscar's words while keeping my eyes laser focused on the street ahead. "What time is the reservation for?" I lick my dry lips again with desperation.

He glances at his watch and sits a little straighter. "Seven p.m. Another ten minutes."

I sit forward in the seat, unable to help chewing the fucking skin on the side of my nail, my leg is bouncing with nervousness. The thought of seeing her again brings forth a mixture of sickness and excitement. A couple of people are milling around, and I scan their faces. I see neither of them is Will as they both enter the restaurant.

Oscar moves closer to the window and points. "There, that's the ex."

I watch the guy who's climbed out of a slick black Porsche Cayenne Turbo. He's tall, around six feet, and lean. Fairly broad shoulders, but not as thick as mine. He's got light-brown hair, shortly cropped at the sides and longer on top. His jaw is chiseled, with a shadow of scruff.

The guy exudes confidence as he straightens his navy three-piece suit. I'll give the guy credit. He looks good. Fucking prick. He stands cross-legged, leaning against his car and texting on his phone.

I glance down at myself. Filthy white T-shirt, ripped denim jeans, and a battered pair of Converse on my feet. I look like a fucking deadbeat compared to this prick.

My eyes snap back up when I see movement come from around the opposite corner. I freeze; my whole body stills at the sight of her. Fuck, she looks incredible. My heart pounds against my chest, the throbbing noise invading my ears. My heart fucking aches, causing me to rub my hand over it.

Long dark hair flows in waves down her back. Fucking sky-high, fuck-me black heels make her legs a mile fucking long. A black pencil skirt sits high-waisted, showing off her smoking-hot body. A short cropped black top with short sleeves gives the slightest tease of her chest with her tits pushed up. Her face is as beautiful as ever, and when she sees Jack, her fucking face lights up. Her smile is enormous. She used to smile like that for me. My heart sinks. I'm so fucking screwed.

Jack turns to greet her and gives a lopsided smile; it looks teasing as he casually walks toward her. She's like an excitable child, making crazy arm gestures toward him that make her look like she's buzzing. Jack laughs at her, then grabs her hands and pulls her into a hug, kissing the top of her head. She nuzzles under his arm as they walk into the restaurant together, and just like that, my fucking mood plummets.

"They're divorced," Oscar states, picking up on my mood.

I push my messy hair from my forehead. "Yeah, they

sure looked happy though." I sound like a pathetic, sulking kid whose toy has been crushed.

"So, what now?" Oscar asks, uncertainty in his voice.

I take a few minutes before answering him. "Now I get some sleep and get showered. Tomorrow, I make a trip to 428 Elm Tree Grove, New Haven, Connecticut."

Oscar tilts his head toward me to confirm he understands my plan.

Chapter Two

Con

The drive here took forever. After barely sleeping last night, my mind is no clearer than it was when I saw her at the restaurant yesterday.

I just need to see her up close. To make sure she's okay. That's what I tell myself, at least. Get answers to my questions about what's been happening in her life, that's all. My hand shakes as I scrub it through my hair.

Bren has driven us here today. I think he's feeling guilty about dropping the bomb in the first place, and this is his way of being supportive. I'm riding shotgun while Cal sits in the back seat. Not sure what he's doing here, but he's probably the most down to earth of my brothers, so maybe that's why he came along? Moral support?

We pull onto Elm Tree Grove. It's a neat, stereotypical suburban street, with large colonial-style homes. Will must love living here; this is something she always wanted. It looks fucking perfect.

The car pulls to a stop directly opposite 428. I don't give either of my brothers a chance to lecture me before I jump out the car, dart across the road, and walk up the drive. I swallow back my anxiety and climb up the steps onto the front porch. Before I can talk myself out of it, I knock loudly on the door. Rocking on my heels, I'm aware that Cal is approaching. He mumbles a subtle "Fuck," but I ignore him, concentrating on the task at hand. Nervous as fuck.

I hear a noise from inside the house and what sounds like someone running down the stairs. The door pulls open, and I'm stunned into silence. Our eyes meet, and what appears to be shock registers in hers. Will stands there directly in front of me. My heart thumps hard against my chest, causing me to wince. I rub at the pain.

I take her in. Her hair is up in a messy bun, a black camisole top slinks off her shoulder with blue paint on it. She wears short cropped jean shorts and navy Converse. She's dotted in blue paint here and there, including her fingers and forehead. I slowly rake my eyes back up to her face. Her face is a blank expression of indifference, although she seems slightly stunned, with her mouth gaping open.

"W-wh-what are you doing here?" She brushes her forehead with the back of her hand.

I glance behind me. Cal is on the lawn, leaning against the porch fence, and Bren has stayed in the car. I swallow thickly, a tremble to my voice. "I … I came to talk to you."

Her chest is flushed and rising faster by the second as we stand there in utter silence staring at one another.

My eyes vaguely register someone striding down the

stairs behind her. Will slowly closes her eyes, deep in thought while trying to regulate her breathing.

"Willow, who's at the——" Before he finishes his sentence, the douche takes the door from Will's hand and opens it wider.

I take in the prick that is her ex-husband. He's shirtless, with low-cut jeans, showing his ripped chest off. Fucking dick. He's also covered in blue paint. The dick still has the paintbrush in his hand. He stares at me, then pokes his head out the door to eye Cal. He sighs, brushes his hand through his hair, and opens the door fully. "You best come in, and your brothers too." He nods in their direction.

Will

"Someone's at the front door," Jack says, nodding toward the open bedroom door. I sigh. Another interruption, great, we'll never get this done.

"Okay. I'll be back in a minute." I place the paintbrush down.

"Yeah. Yeah. Bring drinks back with you." Jack laughs as I head out the door to go downstairs.

My feet hit the stairs quickly, desperate to hurry back and continue. I unlock the front door without checking who's there. God, Jack would kill me for being so reckless. I shake my head at myself.

Turning the handle, I pull the door open, and the life is sucked out of me. There, standing in front of me, is Connor O'Connell.

The son of a bitch is standing on my doorstep. And worse, he looks fucking hot.

My initial shock is put on the back burner as I slowly take him in. Thick dark waves on top of his head, deep-sparkling-blue eyes, and a tanned complexion. His white button-down shirt is pulled tightly across his broad shoulders, his sleeves are rolled up to his elbow, exposing his firm muscled arms. He's wearing fitted black jeans and smart dress shoes. He also smells incredible. Bastard.

I want to say something. I want to say, "Fuck off," but nothing comes out of my traitorous mouth.

"W-wh-what are you doing here?" I stutter like an idiot, then I rub at my forehead in disbelief.

He seems nervous as he shifts from foot to foot. His throat bobs. "I … I came to talk to you."

My mind is blank. I can't think straight. My heart is bursting through my chest, and I feel like I'm going to have a panic attack. He needs to leave; he needs to get the hell out of here and leave us the fuck alone.

I can hear Jack coming down the stairs, and I close my eyes, willing him to go into the kitchen or better yet, back upstairs.

"Willow, who's at the—" His words are cut off as he opens the door wider to see for himself. He tenses beside me and slowly rubs his hand down my back. My shoulders loosen but only slightly.

But then he opens the door wider, surprising the hell out of me, and I could seriously rip his eyes out. He pokes his head out the door, gazing around the property. Then he peers down the street both ways before saying, "You best come in, and your brothers too." He gestures to the black SUV across the road.

What the hell just happened? Seriously, what is he thinking?

I stand there a moment, frozen on the spot. Con moves toward me, and I snap out of my trance and move aside. Next to follow is Cal. I peek up at him, and his lips tighten into an apologetic smile at me. Running across my lawn and straight into my house is Bren, who then bends down and kisses my forehead. "Nice to see you again, Will." I'm once again snapped out of my trance by my childhood nickname "Will." I haven't been Will in a long time. Approximately five years.

"Babe, get over here and sit down. I'll make us some drinks," Jack calls. He's in the living area, where our guests are seated while I'm still standing here with the door open like an idiot.

I spin on my heel. "W-w-what the hell do you think you're doing?" I screech, ignoring everyone but Jack.

Jack glares at me and exhales, then his expression falters and transforms into a fucking patronizingly appeasing smile. "Babe, you need to talk to him." He motions his head toward Con. *Oh, hell no.*

My head throbs, and I press my fingers to my temples. "I don't need to do a damn thing, Jack. What I need is for them to get the hell out of my house!" I point toward the door.

I don't care that my audience can see and hear every damn word. In fact, I'm quite pleased they can. Hopefully, it will encourage them to fuck off!

"Will, listen, I haven't come here to cause any trouble or to upset you—"

His voice grates on me, so I hold my hand up to stop his words. "Then leave. Go on. Get up and go. You're not welcome here!" I point again at the door.

I'm glued to the spot between the open-plan kitchen and the living area. Con is on the sofa, Bren and Cal are on the chairs. Jack is shooting daggers my way from behind the kitchen counter.

"Willow, you're being fucking childish. I'm making us drinks, so sit your ass down and listen." Jack's no-nonsense tone pisses me off. I jump back at his words. He always does this, scorns me like a child. I walk over to the kitchen island and sit on a barstool that puts my back slightly turned away from Con and has me sitting directly in front of Cal.

I glare at Jack, then stare down at my lap and chew the inside of my cheek to stop myself from reacting.

Silence fills the room before Cal clears his throat. "I'm married now with two kids," he announces with a smile, clearly trying to lighten the mood.

I peek up from my lap and toward Cal. His warm eyes and tight smile greet me. How can I be mad at him? "That's really nice, Cal. I'm pleased for you," I say, meaning every word.

"Thanks. My oldest, Reece, he's a fucking handful, but that just makes the good days even more special." We always knew Cal was a softy, but hearing him and seeing the pride shine through his eyes only reinforces how caring he is.

Bren chuckles at Cal's choice of words. "Do you get many special days, Cal?" he jokes.

"Fuck off!" Cal responds, all traces of softness gone.

We all laugh a little, but it's forced.

Jack walks around us and hands the requested drinks out. I must have zoned out because I missed what everyone requested. Silence again. Uncomfortable fucking silence, so my jaw ticks in frustration.

Con clears his throat and straightens his defined shoulders. "You weren't at your father's funeral last year?" he asks. But it's a rhetorical question.

I laugh to myself. "Why the fuck would I want to go to that?" Con's body startles at my words, and his face is one of confusion.

"She hated her dad," Jack jumps in to explain.

"Since when?" Con's eyebrows furrow.

I shake my head. He's been so deluded it's not even funny. "Since always, Con. You were just too blind to see." I sigh and roll my eyes at him.

Jack clears his throat. "Listen, I'm going to have to shoot off …" He raises his brows at me, and I nod in understanding. "I won't be long. You need to talk, Willow. *Explain*." His eyes drill into mine, making me scoff. Jack responds with a sigh while his face drops, full of disappointment. *Well, fuck him.*

He leaves, shutting the front door. When it clicks, I jump back to reality.

"Seems like a nice guy," Bren comments.

"Yeah, he is. He's the best," I boast, holding my head high.

Con scoffs, and I spin to face him. "Something to say, asshole?"

He looks directly at me, appearing frustrated, and licks his lips as if ready to battle. "Yeah, actually, I do. If he's the best, as you proudly say. Why the fuck were you at a domestic abuse survivor's event last week?" His voice rises.

I choke. I genuinely choke. How the hell dare he? I laugh condescendingly. "Do you think Jack's abusive? Is that it? You're kidding me, right? Who the hell do you think you are? What the fuck does it matter to you, anyway? You're unbelievable!" The sound of my voice is increasing along with my temper. I can't get my words out quick enough I'm so damn angry.

Bren speaks up. His tone is explanatory. "I was at the event last week, Will. I mentioned it to Con, and he wanted to check in on you. To make sure everything was okay." He tries to reason with me.

"Check in on me? Are you serious?" My eyes alight with fire, my veins pumping in anger.

"I was trying to do right," Con declares. Oh my fucking God, he did not just say that!

"Do right?" I ask, utterly shocked, my mouth open wide.

He brushes his hand through his hair and quickly looks away. Yeah, fucking guilty.

"Are you okay, Will?" Cal gently coaxes.

"I'm fucking fine, Cal. Fine!" I snap back at him.

I'm so fuming mad right now I can't speak. I take a shaky drink of my water, my hands trembling with rage.

Cal

Con has been quiet all the way here. Anxiety rolling off him in waves, with his leg continuously bouncing, and he can't stop fidgeting. Oscar had explained what terrible shape he was in yesterday, and I want to be here for him today for support. He has a habit of getting himself into more trouble than necessary, and I don't want him to say or do anything he might regret. He's been a wealth of encouragement and support for me over the years, and I need to be the same for him.

As we turn into the streets surrounding Elm Tree Grove, I get uncomfortable. The neighborhood is an idealistic area for families, clean and safe looking. We've recently passed a park; streets are lined with trees, and it looks like something out of a movie scene with white picket fences and perfectly manicured gardens. The houses are large without being ostentatious. It's very clearly a family-oriented neighborhood. One I'm certain my wife, Lily, would love.

As we pull up opposite Will's home, I'm getting a little concerned at the red flags drawing my attention, and my brother is too wrapped up in his own agenda to realize the things staring us in the face.

Such as, the home in which Will lives in is very large for one person. There's also the fact that a minivan is parked in the driveway. Seriously, who the fuck owns a minivan without necessity?

Walking behind Con, I glance down the side of the house. Yeah, a fucking kid's scooter sits propped against the wall of the house. Jesus, this is going to be a shitshow.

Looking up at my eager brother on the front porch, I can only sympathize because he will soon be very disappointed, and I'm fully aware it's going to fucking gut him. I run a frustrated hand through my hair.

When Will's husband lets us into their home, I almost don't want to accept the offer. We're clearly intruding on a very happy family setup.

Straight ahead are stairs with little sneakers at the bottom. I scrub my hand down my face. Fuck, this will be hard.

To our right is a large open-plan living area leading to a large modern kitchen. Jack kindly gestures for us to sit while he makes us drinks. Will is still very dumbfounded, and it would almost be amusing if I hadn't already realized this was going to go tits up.

As we make aimless chit chat, I stand and scan the room. Narrowing in on the family photos adorning the fireplace, I lift one up and instantly spot the little boy. Familiar eyes gleam back at me. *Holy shit.*

Will

The door clicks open far too soon, and Jack returns, causing my stomach to sink. I close my eyes at the impending sound, knowing what's coming next.

"Mommy, I made a picture!"

I wince.

"That's great, buddy. Can you take it upstairs, and I'll pin it up later, okay?" I smile softly in his direction.

"Sure, is my room painted yet?" My son's eager chatter makes my throat bob in anxiety.

Con's back straightens at the sound of my son's voice. His jaw tenses. Luckily, his back is to him, and he doesn't turn to see him. Cal's eyes are trained on Keen. *Shit.*

Jack subtly catches my eye, and I dart my gaze toward the stairs to prompt him. He nods.

"Come on, Keen. Let's go and see how far me and Mommy got with your room, hey?!"

I can see the anger radiating off Con, but I don't want to spare him another look.

As the door at the top of the stairs closes, his tense

jaw loosens and his venomous words spill out. "You named your fucking son Keen?!" His seething glare shoots fire in my direction.

I laugh. "Yeah, Con, I named him Keenan. We call him Keen." I raise my chin.

"How the fuck could you name your son after my dead brother and think that's okay?" His leg is bouncing, waves of tension rolling off him, and his whole body is vibrating.

How dare he? "Why the fuck wouldn't I think it's okay to do that? It wasn't just you that lost him that night, Con. Stop being so goddamn self-centered!" I spit back.

His hand flies around the room. "You're living here in your perfect fucking house, with your perfect fucking family and your fucking perfect husband, with your perfect son named Keenan." He shakes his head in disbelief, venom oozing from his words. The vein at his temple is pulsating. *Yeah, he's beyond pissed.*

Cal gets up slowly and walks toward the dresser against the wall, casually looking around. I'm hoping this means he's getting fed up with the unnecessary visit.

Jack comes back downstairs. "Keen's on his console with his headphones on." My shoulders ease back slightly, and I nod and flash him a tight smile.

"Have you discussed matters?" he asks, gesturing toward Con.

I shake my head slowly. "There's nothing to discuss, Jack. I'm sure Con is getting ready to leave?"

I stare at Con, who is still sitting, silently fuming. His hands are clasped together; the whites of his knuckles evident.

"How old's Keen?" Cal asks.

He fucking knows. My stomach plummets.

My eyes dart toward Jack's, and he speaks up with confidence, ignoring my silent pleas. "He's almost four."

Con's bright-blue eyes dart to mine with shock, embroiled with anger, causing me to take a sudden intake of breath. He gasps dramatically before snarling, "You fucking bitch! You kept the baby and took the money?" he spits out.

My body is stunned by his words. Jack's body tenses, and he points his finger in Con's direction. "Do not fucking call her that, otherwise, I'll put my fucking gun to your head. Do you understand me?!" he shouts back at Con.

Before Con can respond, Bren jumps in. "What baby? What money?"

I glance toward Bren and shake my head with a small laugh at Con's audacity.

"You've no fucking clue what you're talking about, Con. Unless you want all your dirty little secrets exposed, I suggest you get the hell out of my house and don't come back!" I snipe, noticing his face is paler than the flush red he was previously radiating.

"What the fuck did you do?" Cal spins on his heels and away from the photograph's lining the dresser to face Con.

He doesn't answer. *Coward.*

"I asked you a question, Connor. Fucking answer me!" he demands louder.

Con sighs and brushes his hand through his hair. "I assumed she'd gotten rid of the baby." He swallows thickly, his voice low. "Clearly, she didn't," Con mutters while throwing his arm out toward the stairs. Toward Keen.

Jack is still rigid, standing beside me in his silently supportive manner.

Cal turns toward me, his eyebrows quirked upward. Jack nods at me in encouragement.

I take a deep breath. "What he's trying to say, Cal, is he gave me two thousand dollars in cash to go and have an abortion. Against my wishes, I must add." I raise my chin with determination to be truly heard.

Cal gasps, and Con drops his head in his hands in shame. In the quickest move I've ever seen, Bren lunges out of his chair and flies at Con, who looks up and doesn't see the punch to his jaw coming. "Fuck!" Con screeches in the aftermath. "Motherfucker." He works his jaw from side to side. Bren paces back and forth, his face red with anger.

Jack silently pours Bren a whiskey and hands it to him, presumably to calm him down, then Bren sits in the chair, emptying the glass and glaring at Con, who is rubbing his jaw with a wince.

Cal is standing in front of Con with his hands on his hips, seething. "Let me get this straight. You gave your teenage girlfriend two thousand dollars to abort your baby? And you're pissed because she didn't do it?"

"I'm pissed because she kept it from me," he sneers back while glaring at me. I stare him down.

Jack breaks the tension. "How could you leave a teenage girl to deal with that shit by herself? To walk in there and have to deal with losing a baby by herself? You couldn't even be man enough to be there for her. I don't understand how the fuck you sleep at night." Jack's disgust seeps from him in waves as he shakes his head at Con.

Con hangs his head in shame. Well, motherfucker, here comes your next bombshell.

My spine straightens with confidence as I stand and approach him. "Well, I went as per your strict instructions, Con. I obeyed your request. Especially after the whole, 'I don't want a family with you ever and I don't even want to be with you, Will,' speech." I make finger quotes at the latter, as his words come back to me with vengeance. He winces as I repeat them.

"Unfortunately for you, I was too far along in the pregnancy, Con." My throat clogs as the emotions grip me like it was yesterday. Gently, I shake my head, not wanting to share the worst day of my life with them, but I know I have to. I have to make them believe I tried to do what he said was best. I trusted him.

I struggle to breathe through the tears. "They said I was nearly five months pregnant, and they wouldn't terminate at that point. I'd spent all goddamn morning building the courage up to go, and when I got there, they couldn't do it." A sob catches in my throat. "I tried, you bastard, I fucking tried. While you were off enjoying yourself like the selfish prick you are, I was trying to kill my baby! So don't you dare come in here and rip me and my life apart for making the best of things. And don't you dare attack Jack for manning up and being a father figure to Keen. Don't you fucking dare." I point my finger at him while shaking. My heart thrashes violently against my chest, and my hands shake from anger.

Con bends forward with his head in his hands. I have zero sympathy.

My breathing is frantic as I battle with my emotions of being both angry and upset.

"Will, are you okay?" Cal murmurs.

I shake my head. "No, Cal, I'm not okay. Do you know what happened next, Con?" His blurry eyes meet mine, and I stare through his saddened blues and continue on. Of course, he doesn't know what happened next. The bastard wouldn't know because he didn't care.

"I went home terrified, with the two thousand dollars stuffed in my hoodie. My father waiting for me in his chair with a bottle half empty in his hands."

I close my eyes as the nightmare scene comes back to me. Jack takes ahold of my hand, and Cal's eyes flit to it. I gulp and continue. "He was waiting for me. One of his little minions had reported back to him where I'd been ..."

"Fuck" comes from Bren. He drags his hand down his face. It was common knowledge my father was strict and had a vicious temper. It's part of the reason Con and I would sneak around.

"He knew. Knew I'd been for an abortion. He knew I was too far gone for one. He got up and picked the metal poker up. I was so fucking scared. His eyes were glazed and black, they were soulless. He called me a slut, a whore. The usual." Con seems genuinely surprised, so fucking oblivious. I shake my head at his naivety.

"He hit me and hit me until I fell. He said if they couldn't get rid of the baby, he would! He hit me with that fucking poker until I stopped screaming."

"Jesus!" Cal stares at me with sympathy and disgust in his eyes.

"A few more kicks to the stomach made me make a god-awful noise. I felt a gush, and when he saw the blood between my legs on my jeans, he gave a satisfied grunt, slammed the door, and left. I was lifeless. My body wouldn't move. It went beyond pain. I couldn't feel a single thing."

The room is silent as I swipe the tears from my eyes. They're watching me, waiting for me to continue. To answer the unanswered questions. I take a drink of my water, and Jack squeezes my hand in support.

"Milo, my brother, came home. You know what he did? He picked me up. Told me I asked for this, how it was my own fault. He drove me to the hospital and laid me down outside the doors. He bent down and whispered in my ear, 'And don't fucking come back, whore.'"

Cal winces at my words. Bren's fists are clamped together, and Con's expression is empty, void of anything.

I clear my throat and chuckle. "So, yeah, Con. I guess I kept your baby and your money," I sneer.

Jack brushes up alongside me and tucks my hair behind my ears. "You did good, babe. I'm proud of you." He kisses my forehead. Con's eyes drill into me.

I swallow thickly. "I was treated for broken ribs, wrist, cheekbone, among other things. At the hospital, I was given a cervical stitch to hold the baby in place. I was underage, so the hospital put me under CPS, in a program for Domestic Abuse Survivors. They help you get on your feet while keeping your circumstances hidden. As far as I'm aware, my family thought I lost the baby. He came premature, his lungs weren't fully developed at the time. Eventually, we were moved into a small condo supported by the program. I used the money you gave me for his crib and furnishings. So yeah, thanks for the abortion money, Con," I say, rolling my eyes, with tears blurring my vision.

"Fuck, I didn't know, Will!" he pleads. His hands are

shaking in his lap, his face white, and desperation etches his handsome features.

I roll my eyes and stifle a laugh, determined not to sympathize with him. "You're right, you didn't know. But you didn't care either, did you?"

He says nothing; he can't deny it. It's the truth and he knows it.

Cal breaks the silence. His face a picture of fury. "I'm so fucking ashamed of you right now, Con. So fucking ashamed." He shakes his head.

"Don't you think I'm ashamed of myself?" he desperately tries to argue.

"It's not fucking about you, is it?" Bren snaps.

"No. You're right, it's not." His voice is low, and he's visibly shaking. "What happens now, Will?"

Oh, you've got to be fucking kidding me. "You leave! Do what you're good at. You turn your back, and you go!" I screech back to him, pointing at the door.

"No!" Jack and Cal say together.

My eyes dart to Jack's, and I scowl at him. He tries to placate me. "Babe, you know that's not a good idea."

I shake my head, my jaw tense. Un-fucking-believable.

"Will, even if we left here today with no intentions of coming back, you understand it's not safe, you know we have enemies," Cal explains calmly.

I gasp at the realization, a tremor rippling through my body, with a new anger settling in. "So, you bastards show up at my door and bring your fucking enemies to me? To us? That's what you're saying?"

Con winces at my words. He knows I'm right. They just opened the door to destroy our lives.

Chapter Three

Con

Will sinks into her chair after dropping one hell of a bombshell on us. On me.

I feel sick to my stomach. How the fuck did I miss this? How the fuck did I let this happen? And now I have a fucking son?

I can't stop the tremble in my body. I want to sob like a fucking baby. Jesus, I'm such a pathetic screwup. What the fuck have I done?

Jack's hands are tender on Will, rubbing up and down her back.

His hands brush delicately over my girl's body. With hate for him coursing through my body, my jaw locks. My hands should be there. My fucking hands should be rubbing her back, soothing her.

Bren's watching me with a razor-sharp glare. They fucking hate me. All of them do. I can sense it; I don't fucking blame them.

Jesus. I scrub a hand down my face. I hate myself.

Jack's voice is calm. "Listen, I've ordered some pizzas for dinner. Perhaps you guys can stay, and when Keen goes to bed, we can discuss this a little more?"

Will scoffs. "You cannot be serious, Jack? You've just heard them; they've fucked up our entire lives showing up here. And now you want us to play happy fucking families and chat?"

Jack's body bristles at her words. "I want what's best for you and Keen. You both need to be kept safe, and at the moment, these guys can do that." He scans over us in approval.

Will walks around the kitchen counter and gets plates out, obviously busying herself to avoid us. The loud clatter of plates is a clear sign of how pissed she is.

"Who do we tell Keen we are?" Cal asks.

"Friends!" Will snaps back over her shoulder.

Fuck that, if I'm a fucking father, I'm going to be one.

"I'm his dad, Will," I plead.

Her eyes narrow on me. "No, you are not. You didn't want to be one, remember? You're not just going to walk in here and think you can take over my family and everything I've built. Keen needs structure and stability. Not some self-centered, self-absorbed prick in his life." I wince at her harsh words.

"Will, enough. I'm sure Con is going to want to prove himself to you and Keen?" Jack asks with a raised eyebrow at me.

"Of course." I nod in agreement with him. I'm desperate for any connection she's prepared to give.

"In which case, perhaps we introduce you all as friends. Once Will is comfortable for you to be something more, when you've proven yourself to be something more, then perhaps have another discussion about who you're going to be to Keen?" How the fuck do I argue with that? Still don't like the fucking know-it-all prick, though.

"I think that's for the best. Con's got a lot to prove. We understand your concerns, Will. But I can assure you that we're your family now. You and Keen will have us in your life, and no matter what happens with Con, we aren't going anywhere."

Well, cheers for the vote of fucking confidence, Cal. I shake my head at him. He doesn't think I'm capable or deserving, my own fucking brother.

"Thank you, Cal. That means a lot." Her voice is gentle, like the Will I remember. The Will I'm desperate for.

————

Before long I hear small footsteps coming down the stairs, and I take a deep breath to turn around and face him. My son.

I turn slowly, but where I look, he isn't there. He's way smaller than I expected, and he takes my breath away. He's barely above the height of the banister, and when his small feet hit the floor, I get a proper opportunity to see him. Keen's small and thin. My chest tightens and I gasp. His brown hair is thick like mine, wavy, and he has big blue eyes. He's my fucking double. I stare back at Cal and Bren open-mouthed, my eyes asking them if they're seeing it too. They both dip their heads at me, and I'm overcome with emotion. I choke on a quiet sob and quickly try to mask it with a cough. Fuck, I need to pull myself together. I brush my hands down my jeans uncomfortably.

"Hey, Keens. Come and say hello to Mommy's friends." Will holds her hand out for Keen, and he goes to her. He's wearing little joggers and a T-shirt with a tiger on the front, cute as fuck.

She points. "This one here is Cal." Cal bends down to Keen and shakes his little hand; Keen tries to move behind Will. "This big guy is Bren." Keen laughs at Will's description of Bren. Bren moves forward and fist bumps Keen. This earns him another chuckle. He's so fucking cute.

Will's body straightens as she approaches me. I swear to Christ, I can sense the tension and hate radiating off her. "This is Con."

I get down on my knees so I'm level with him. His blue eyes meet mine, and I smile softly. I must look a mess. "Hi, Keen, it's good to meet you." He peeks at me from behind Will's leg. I'm unsure what to do or say. "I like your T-shirt, dude. Do you like tigers?"

Keen steps forward a little, his voice timid. "I like all animals. My mommy's going to take me to the zoo when it's my birthday and I turn four." He holds up four fingers. I chuckle at how fucking clever my little man is.

"Wow. Dude, that sounds amazing. I bet they have tigers there; do you think I could come?" I lick my lips and stare up at Will, hoping she can see the promise in my eyes. Say fucking yes. Please say yes.

"I'll have to ask my mommy." This makes me laugh, Bren and Cal too.

The doorbell rings, breaking the small conversation and cutting the tension.

Jack answers the door and walks back into the kitchen area with a pile of pizza boxes.

"Yes!" Keen declares, jumping up with his little fist in the air.

"Jack, did you get Coke too?" His little face is alight, and I don't miss the fact he called Jack by his first name, and relief rolls through me.

Earlier, I had wondered if he called him dad. I sink into the chair, smiling internally. I've not lost them yet. No fucking way.

"Yeah, buddy, I got Coke too." A wide grin graces Keen's face as he smiles up at Jack. My gut fucking clenches, my hopeful mood turning sour.

"Wow. You must be a big boy if your mommy lets you have Coke, Keen." Cal laughs, probably thinking about his teenage son, Reece, who is banned from drinking Coke.

"I am. I can have Coke on special days, can't I, Mommy?"

"Yes, that's right, sweetheart." Will gives Keen a solemn smile as she sets about dishing the pizza out.

Will hands me a plate with pepperoni pizza on it. It's my favorite, and she's clearly remembered. Or was it a fucking coincidence? "Thanks." She gives me a fake smile back, clearly playing nice.

Everyone digs in, eating and drinking. Brief conversations around Keen occur as both Bren and Cal ask questions about Will and Keen. I zone out and just watch the interaction. I can't take my eyes off Keen. Will has done so well with him. He's chatty, cute, and funny. The kid is fucking adorable. He even eats his pizza like me, peeling off the pepperoni and then saving the pieces until last. Will's demeanor is damn right defensive. She's pissed. I try not to stare at her, but I can't fucking help it. I'm like a magnet, drawn to her without even trying.

Inside, I tell myself to remain silent. I'm fucking scared what she will say if I speak, and I sure as fuck don't want her throwing us out anytime soon.

We've just finished eating when Will stands. "Keen, come on, buddy, it's way past your bedtime. Let's go and get you tucked in bed with a quick story tonight. Are you going to say goodbye to our friends?" Shit, I don't want them to leave the fucking room. I turn to Cal for help, but he's talking to Jack.

Keen runs to Jack for a hug, and when he picks him up, Keen wraps his arms around his neck. "Night, night, little man. I'll see you soon, okay?" Fuck, that's crushing. Standing, I rub my hand through my hair, unable to watch the scene in front of me. I walk to the window and stare out of it, swallowing back the thickness in my throat.

"Night, night, Jack, love you," he says back. I rub at the pain in my chest and wince. Unable to breathe, I close my eyes and count.

Behind me, my brothers say their goodnights, but I don't turn around to see.

"Night, Keen," I grunt out. It fucking pains me not to turn toward him. I don't want to say goodbye, but then I don't want him to think I didn't wish him a good night's sleep either. I'm so fucking screwed.

As soon as I hear Keen's door close, I turn around to face my brothers and Jack.

Jack's words are quick and terse. "Listen, I understand this is hard for you, Con." I scoff. *What the fuck does he know?* "But I really need you all to help keep them safe." My spine straightens; it feels like there's an innuendo there.

Bren picks up on it too, and his eyes narrow at Jack. "What aren't you telling us, Jack?" His voice stern with a warning behind it.

Jack exhales and sits in a chair. "Since meeting Willow, I had a friend of mine keep a close eye on her family in New Jersey. I didn't trust that they wouldn't come after her. I genuinely believe they think Willow lost Keen. I wasn't going to put it past them to try to make sure she keeps her mouth shut about what happened. "

"Anyway, when Willow's father passed away, her brother, Milo, took a more sinister role in the business." He fidgets with his hands. We're all well aware of Milo. We have been for several years. He's into dealing drugs and has been working closely with a gang of Russians on the outskirts of the city. They're ruthless and are virtual outlaws compared to other gangs.

Jack continues. "About six months ago, my friend contacted me to say Milo had registered Willow on a missing person site. He's also been paying a private investigator in New Jersey." Jack's vein in his temple is throbbing, anger radiating from his body. "The function that we attended last week, someone took photographs of the sponsors and spokespersons. Something that isn't supposed to happen at these events, ever!" He grits out the last word.

I drop into the chair. *Shit.*

"Milo is currently under investigation in both our jurisdictions, and I'm hoping the case against him will be enough to put him away for life. But in the meantime, he's a fucking walking time bomb."

"She can't stay here!" I declare, almost surprising myself.

"Agreed," Bren states without hesitation.

Jack fidgets with his hands. "I completely fucking agree with you but …" He shakes his head and stares up to the ceiling. "Willow's fucking stubborn, and the feelings she harbors toward you, Con, I don't mean any disrespect, but she's well within her rights to feel that way about you."

"I know." I fucking know. Shame courses through me, and I rub my hand through my hair in annoyance with myself.

"They can stay with me," Bren suggests. Fuck that. My family isn't staying with him. They're fucking mine.

"Like fuck they are. They're my fucking family, not yours. Get your own," I spit back at him.

"I didn't think you wanted a family, Con?" Cal challenges.

"Fuck off, and stop being a dick. They're here now, aren't they? If they're going anywhere, they're going with me!" I stab my finger into my chest for emphasis.

With Milo openly seeking Will out and with our own enemies, they sure as shit aren't safe living here unprotected.

My gut clenches at the thought of someone hurting either of them.

Chapter Four

Will

Tiptoeing down the stairs, I approach the bottom step and listen to their hushed voices. I'm surprised at how close Jack is standing with them, because he is very clearly not their biggest fan. The hairs on the back of my neck prick up. Why do I get the sense they're conspiring?

I walk into the room, and the fuckers scurry away from one another. "What the hell's going on?" I ask while crossing my arms over my chest.

Jack's demeanor screams tension, and Con appears a bag of nerves. Cal shuffles from foot to foot. "We think it's best if you guys come and stay with us for a little while."

My voice catches in my mouth, and I let out a surprised laugh. *Is he fucking serious?* "No! Absolutely not."

"Goddamn it, Willow. Will you just listen to

reason?!" Jack snaps, making me jump. His fists tighten beside him, completely unlike him.

I can see the stress and concern written all over his face. "What aren't you telling me, Jack?"

He has the fucking nerve to glance at the others before bringing his eyes back to mine and deciding to be honest. "I have intel, Willow. Intel that concerns me. It's about your and Keen's safety."

"What kind of intel?" I swallow deeply, a lump forming in my throat.

"Does it fucking matter?" His voice rises in irritation.

Jack doesn't lose his temper very often, and it's rare he speaks out of line to me. But yeah, it matters. Of course, it fucking does.

"You're wanting to uproot me and Keen from our home, Jack, from our lives. Of course it fucking matters."

"Milo." As soon as the name leaves his mouth, I struggle to stand. My chest feels tight, and I can't seem to catch my breath. Jack senses the change in me and helps me to sit down. "I'm so sorry, babe, if there was something I could do, I would. I swear." His voice is sad and desperate.

"You're the fucking police, Jack." I can't help but point that out.

He ducks his head. "I know. But I can't be here twenty-four seven, and I genuinely think he would run fucking shit scared if he thought you were being protected by Con and his family. Fuck, he'd probably drop the whole little vendetta he's got going on in his head altogether. As you're aware, I've been investigating his activity for a while; well, we're getting closer to finding him. Until then, you and Keen need to lie low."

"How long?"

He watches me with a confused expression. "How long what?"

"How long do I have to stay with them, Jack?" My voice is sharper. I'm fucking pissed.

Con shifts in his chair, squirming.

"I'm not sure. He's currently MIA, fuck knows where he is. But if you stay with Con and the guys, I can concentrate on the investigation. The sooner I do that, the sooner the restraints on you loosen."

"Restraints? I'm not a fucking dog or a criminal, Jack!" Jesus, his delivery needs some serious work.

I slowly take in everything he's said. The room sits in silence, watching the exchange. We're in danger. I glance at Con, who's watching me with a painful intensity, and clench my jaw.

"We can protect you, Will. Let us help you. You've always been part of our family, and nothing's changed. Keen added into the mix is a blessing, Will. We'll love and protect him. Fuck, our Ma's going to be buzzing." Bren's words resonate with me, and I begrudgingly smile.

Cyn, Con's mom, loves kids. She always showered me with love and affection. Welcoming me into their home, I'd spend hours with her, taking any excuse not to return home to my living hell. We'd bake together, and she'd tell me how much she wished she could have had a daughter. How having sons, she knew she'd lose them to their "business."

Cyn understood and maybe knew a little about what was going on at home, because she was always so sweet, compassionate and, quite frankly, she mothered me. It was a relationship we both embraced. She never asked me about our relationship, but she wasn't blind. She knew; they all did.

"Okay. So where do we stay?" I rub my hands up my arms, suddenly feeling helpless and vulnerable. I've not felt like this in a long time, and it isn't me. There's no way I can go back to that. I shake the feeling off.

"With me," Con states while standing, as if he's about to go to battle and will need to come up with a verbal defense.

I splutter on my words. "With you? Seriously?"

Cons voice exudes confidence. "Absolutely. I want to get to know my son, Will. There's plenty of room in my apartment. You can have as much space as you need. I get a relationship with my son and you both get the protection you need in return."

"Makes sense," Jack agrees. My eyes dart to him with a scowl. The fucking traitor! "It's for the best, Will. Go upstairs and pack some basics. Leave all devices here. You take nothing that can be traced, okay?" He looks at me pointedly.

I stand and nod at his instructions, stunned at the turn of events.

Con

Will's in fucking shock. Like literally in shock. If I didn't want her as much as I do, I'd feel fucking guilty. But the selfish bastard in me is pleased she's coming to stay with me. Shit, she even agreed to it without an argument. That went so much easier than expected.

I sense her enter the room without hearing her; it's something I've always been able to do with her, and it's the only time I'm relaxed. When she's near me, with me.

I need to make her see that she doesn't need to leave when that little shit Milo is handled. I need her to see what she used to see. Apart from all the shit I put her through and the fact I was a selfish little prick, which I'd happily admit right now.

Bren stands, and he takes the two bags from Will before turning and walking out the door with Jack in tow.

"He's strapping Keen's car seat into the vehicle," Cal informs me, looking at the door.

Will is leaning against the wall at the bottom of the stairs, her head down and her arms wrapped around her middle. She looks so lost. I contemplate going over to her; I just need to touch her. Brushing my hair from my eyes, I decide to man the fuck up and check on her.

"Hey." Yeah, nice one, Con.

She lifts her head slightly and stares deep into my eyes, something she's tried to avoid all night. Her eyes are haunted, broken. My heart hammers against my chest as I scan her face. She's pale, her lip quivers, tear tracks mar her face, and she's wearing a vulnerable, vacant expression that makes my gut twist. I've done this. I've given her this haunted, destroyed look.

Her whole demeanor a reminder of the night I told her to get rid of the baby, the night I told her I didn't want her anymore.

The acknowledgment within me makes my body jolt. I swallow thickly, the realization of the hurt I cause just being around her almost brings me to my knees. I'm a selfish bastard, and I hate myself for it, but not nearly as much as she hates me.

I'm not sure how long we stand there staring at one another, but it sure as hell feels like a lifetime. I open my mouth to speak, but before I get the chance, Jack beats me to it.

He surges between us and holds Will's chin in his grasp. "Hey, are you okay? You're going to be okay." He scans her up and down as if checking for something out of place. She sags into him, and he tugs her tighter, his arms wrapping around her waist. When he places a gentle kiss on her forehead, she raises her head and smiles gently at him. I fucking hate it.

My fists clench beside me. He's come between us and obliterated my intentions, and now she's looking at him like some sort of hero. My jaw clenches as I watch on like a fucking dumb creeper.

"Car's ready!" Bren's voice booms, breaking the moment. I spin my head toward his deep voice, and he gives me a sly grin, his lip curling up slightly, and winks at me before turning his back and walking back toward the door. He interrupted the moment on purpose. How long was he standing there?

Did he do that for me? Why would he do that?

Will

I break away from the comfort and safety of Jack's arms. He moves from my side to speak with Cal. It's only then I realize Con is still standing there, watching me with sympathy. Guilt even? I swallow and avert my gaze, not wanting to address his demeanor, not when he's caused all of this.

As we move out onto the porch, I overhear Jack and Cal discussing how they intend to keep in contact with one another.

The screeching sound of brakes rocks the peaceful air surrounding us. In a flash, a black SUV lowers its windows, and before we know what's happening, someone from inside the vehicle opens fire at us. Before my mind can summon any movement, I'm pushed back toward the door into the entrance of my home by Con, his body my shield.

I stumble backward as Jack covers Con with his own body.

Gunshots and shouting boom around us as Cal and Bren retaliate with their own weapons. My heart pounds when I realize the jolts of Jack's body against Con are from bullets hitting him repeatedly.

I gasp when Con's body falls hard against me, a blanket of cover protecting me. Scanning his features, I panic. Did they hit him too?

"I'm okay, Will. Are you okay?"

Did I say it out loud or did Con see the question on my face? I nod frantically as I push him off me.

He moves quickly, and we turn in tandem toward Jack. Con grasps my hands and pushes them against a bloodied chest wound, then quickly tears his shirt over his head to use as a compress.

He walks toward the door with his back against the wall, his hand raised as if telling me to stay put.

I shake myself off from the initial shock and quickly survey Jack. He's breathing heavily, with blood seeping from his chest and another wound in his shoulder.

My lip trembles. "Why did you do that?" Why did he shield Con?

My trembling hands press harder on his chest, causing him to suck in his breath. Slowly, Jack brings his hand to my face. "Because you need him, Willow. You just don't realize how much yet." I glance away from him, scared to acknowledge his words. Scared to admit Jack cares enough about me to not want Con hurt. "You need him." He smiles softly at me, his handsome face grimacing in pain.

Tears pour down my face.

Chapter Five

Con

Cal approaches the door first. "Jack took two bullets. He's stable." He dips his head in acknowledgment.

"Bren's going to wait by the car. We need to get out of here," he pants, looking over his shoulder at Will and Jack on the floor.

Will is distraught beside Jack, so I brush my hand through my hair. There's no way she's going to leave him like that.

As if hearing my thoughts, she says, "I'm not leaving him!" Her voice trembles.

Cal and I walk toward Jack, and he's trying to shuffle something from underneath him. "My phone," he pants.

I delve into his ass pocket and hand him his phone. He quickly sends a text. "My partner Stan … will be here in five minutes with medics. Get Keen and *go!*" His voice is stern, leaving no room for argument.

Cal takes off up the stairs. Willow stares at him

blankly, causing Jack's lips to straighten. "Willow, do as I fucking ask before someone else gets hurt. I'll contact you tomorrow. Now get the fuck out." He struggles to breathe as he kicks the words out, but they have the desired effect on Will. She gingerly backs away from him, and I move around her to help her up.

Before I reach her arms, she descends on him again and presses a hard chaste kiss to his lips. "I love you." Jack's face softens at her words, and he ducks his head timidly at her.

I guide her stunned body to the car, with my hand digging into her waist to stabilize her.

After tucking her in beside me in the back of the SUV, I strap her in like a helpless child. Tears drip from her shocked face.

Keen is already strapped inside, sound asleep. Fuck, the kid can sleep through a hurricane, by the look of him. I'm not sure whether to be in awe or envious. The thought makes me chuckle to myself as we pull away from the side of the road.

———

Cal and Bren share muffled words in the front as Cal brings the phone to his ear, no doubt calling Oscar.

I tune my brothers out and turn toward Will. Her trembling hands pull a blanket higher on Keen's sleeping body, but she quickly drops them into her lap, as if only just realizing they're covered in blood.

Before she has time to contemplate those thoughts, I unlock her seatbelt and pull her toward me. Palming her head, I push her to rest on my bare chest, leaving my hand in her hair to keep her head in place. I'm not sure if I'm trying to comfort her or me.

Her tense body loosens as she crumbles into me with heart-wrenching sobs, and her hands grip my waist as she clings to me, causing my chest to tighten. I never want to let her go.

Cal turns his head and peers back at us, then gives me an approving tilt of his head before facing forward and giving us some privacy.

I nuzzle into her hair, capturing her familiar scent. Vanilla and lemon. My eyes squeeze closed at the memories, emotion racing through me. I band my arms tighter around her, ensuring she can't move away, can't leave me.

Will's tears hit my chest, and the sounds emitting from her rip my heart open, causing a lone tear to trail down my cheek. I never thought I'd see her again, let alone hold her. My heart pounds against her. I'm never letting her go.

Never again.

Will

At some point during the drive, Con's hold on me loosened. I could move away from him and continue my fight against him, my hatred, but I need him. I need his strength and support. I need him to be everything he wasn't, maybe everything he isn't. My arms drop at my thoughts.

"Don't." His voice is stern with a little desperation to it.

I tilt my head to peek up at him, his beautiful blue eyes shining with emotion. "Whatever you were thinking, don't. Please."

His soft voice is a plea. His eyes hold such vulnerability he looks utterly broken. How can the man I fell in love with, the hard-talking joker who showed little genuine emotion, seem so broken? I swallow thickly.

"Please, Will." His hands squeeze me again as I realize he needs me. I nod in agreement and bury my face back in his chest.

Con kisses my head, whispering, "Thank you." I

clutch him so he knows I heard him. His hand brushes lazily up and down my back.

———

We pull into an underground car park, and the lights come on automatically as the car descends farther inside. "Won't they have tracked our car?" I ask, bolting upright in panic, my eyes darting around us.

Cal's commanding voice fills the car. "Maybe. But the car is clear of bugs and trackers. It's likely they're aware this is our car by now. So, if they were coming for you, Will, they know you're here."

My body tenses at Cal's words, causing me to involuntarily whimper.

"Shhh, it's okay, Will. We've got you. We've also got the best security available; I swear it." He brushes his hand up and down my back gently, coaxing the tension from me.

"Come on, let me get you both settled." He opens the door, and I follow him out, taking his hand, his slick muscular body greeting me. Fuck, he needs to put a shirt on.

Cal unstraps Keen with ease; I smile at the fact he is a well-practiced daddy. We follow behind Bren as we enter the elevator. "We're the third apartment from the top. Finn is above us, and Bren has the top floor," Con informs me as he pulls me by my waist into him. Keen is resting his head on Cal's shoulder, completely zonked out, a trail of drool building there.

———

We enter Con's apartment, and when he switches the lights on, my eyes dart around the room. It's a modern, open-plan concept, which would be appealing, but the place is a shithole.

My body stills beside him as I take in the trash strewn across the room; it looks like a party took place at some point and he never got around to cleaning it. Empty takeaway cartons, upturned furniture, and broken glasses.

Then, right there on the kitchen counter, an open foil with white powder.

I gasp. What the actual fuck?

I spin toward him, accusing eyes drilling into his.

Con

As soon as the light illuminates the room, I tense. I'd forgotten how I left the apartment. Obviously, I didn't intend to bring Will back here quite so soon, and I sure as shit didn't expect to bring my son here.

Will freezes beside me, taking in the room the same time as we do. I quickly dart my eyes to the kitchen counter and internally groan at the open cocaine on display. There's no chance Bren will miss that; that man can sniff out anything.

"They're not staying here!" Cal spits the words out, not caring if he disturbs Keen. His body solid with anger, the vein on his neck pumping.

"Damn fucking right they're not. They can stay at my apartment." Bren's shoulders broaden further, like he's ready for a fight. The disgust on their faces is evident. The sickening sensation of failure in my stomach is all too familiar, making my body shake with panic at losing them already. I lick my lips as my throat goes desperately dry.

I don't want them to go anywhere. They're my fucking family. Mine.

If they leave now, will they stay with Bren indefinitely? How would I prove myself? Would Will make me a part-time dad who sees his kid when she decides, and I have no say? Would I even be allowed to see him?

With drugs involved, they have every reason not to. My family would side with Will. I know they would. But I need them. The thought of losing her all over again is too much to bear. My legs feel like they're going to buckle. My heart pounds rapidly as panic floods my veins.

"No," I spit the words out harshly. "I'll clean it up. It won't happen again. I swear. Will, please, by the time you wake up, it'll all be gone. I swear. Please just give me a chance. I want you here, both of you. Please." Will's hazel eyes meet mine; she looks torn, probably wondering what the right thing to do is.

She looks at Keen, then back at me. I bite my lip and brush my hand through my hair, anxiety reeling off me. "Please, Will." I'm hoping she can see the sincerity in my eyes, the desperation in my voice.

Her eyes flit back and forth over my face, likely seeing how pathetic and desperate I am.

She gently nods. "Don't make me regret this. It needs to be right by morning."

I nod frantically, eagerly, before letting out a deep sigh of relief.

"Where should we … erm, where should we sleep?" Will stands with her arms around her middle, hugging herself, the blood still coating her hands. I want to hold her, pull her into me. I stop myself, knowing I'd be rejected.

I swallow thickly and avert my eyes. "Cal, can you show Will where the spare room is? There are fresh towels in the closet." Cal gestures for Will to follow him as he steers her and Keen to the spare room.

"You sure it's suitable in there?" Bren's deep, uncertain voice breaks my thoughts.

I brush my hand through my hair. "Yeah, it's suitable." I don't dare to look at him, and instead, survey the room, staring at all the work that needs done. Shit, it's going to be a long ass night.

"You got a problem?" Bren tips his head toward the cocaine on the counter, cutting into my thoughts.

I dart my eyes to hi. "No, man, I don't. I just use it occasionally when I party." I shrug as if it's no big deal, but let's face it, I know it's a big fucking deal.

"Party?" His eyes bore into mine, as if he's trying to dive into my soul, searching for a lie.

I make sure my voice is confident and hold his eyes. "Clearly, I won't be doing any of that again. So, no need to worry about it." Bren dips his head, satisfied with my response.

Footsteps on the marble floor draw my eyes toward Cal. "What the fuck, Con! This place is a fucking shithole. You can't have drugs around kids, for Christ's sake." Yeah, he thinks I'm that dumb. He stands there with his hands on his hips, seething.

His eyes narrow on me and he exhales. "What the hell happened to Maureen?"

I scoff; he means our cleaner. "Her name was Brenda, and she was a whiney bitch, so I fired her."

"Well, perhaps you need to rethink that decision?" His eyes rove over the room again.

I blow out a deep breath. "Ya think?"

Cal nods, clearly missing my sarcasm. "Will and Keen are settling in. Come on, I'll help you clean, and get rid of that shit." He tilts his head toward the drugs.

"Oh, and tomorrow, we're going to have to tell Da."

"Fuck." My stomach plummets, yet another disappointment for them.

Fuck. My. Life.

Chapter Six

Con

I crashed on the couch a couple of hours ago, grateful yet again for my brother's help.

The sun seeps through the window blinds, and the soft creak of Will's bedroom door alerts me it's definitely morning.

I shoot up and scan the room. We did an amazing job in a few hours. Cal told me he would organize a team of cleaners to come this afternoon to give it a thorough clean, and a team to childproof the apartment. He's like a kid whisperer nowadays, so I'm grateful for his help.

Listening for her footsteps, I don't hear them, so I rise from the couch and make my way past the kitchen counter toward the hallway leading to Will's room.

Just as I approach the hall, I almost stumble over Keen. With the dim lighting and his size, I almost wipe the poor kid out.

He gasps, probably scared shitless.

"Oh, shit." I clamp my mouth closed as quick as I opened it. You're not suppose to swear around kids. *Fuck.*

Keen giggles, pointing his finger at me. "You said a naughty."

I crouch down beside him. "Yeah, I did. Sorry about that, little man." I clear my throat. "You remember me?" My voice shakes with vulnerability, but hopefully, my kid doesn't notice. Although, I bet he's smart, just like Will.

He scrunches his nose up. He looks cute as hell. His wavy hair is a mess, and his hands fidget in front of him. "You're Mommy's friend."

I grin at him; my little dude is fucking clever. "Yeah, my name's Con. You remember?" I nod encouragingly.

He bows his little head. "I did a pee-pee."

I stare at him, a little shocked. Where the fuck did that come from?

Scanning his body, my eyes land on his little tiger pajamas, and they're soaked.

Shit, what the fuck do I do? I tug on my hair in a bit of a panic, then take a deep breath and steel myself; I need to man the fuck up and show everyone I can do this.

I soften my tone so he knows he's not in trouble. "Okay, little man. Do you need a diaper change?"

He wrinkles his nose, then straightens his little shoulders with confidence. "Nope. I don't wear diapers because I'm a big boy. Big boys don't wear diapers, they pee in the potty."

O-kay, then. I scan his face, unsure if he's joking. His face is impassive as he stands proudly. Nope, he's fucking serious. I mean, clearly, he's not a big boy because he pissed his pants but … what. The. Fuck. Ever. I'm sure as shit not going to have my kid upset with me.

"Okay, so we need to change you, right?" Completely unsure if that's what we need to be doing right now.

"Yep." He rocks back and forth on his feet, grinning.

"Okay, little man. Should I bathe you or something?"

"Yep. With bubbles."

"Bubbles, right, got ya." Do I even have fucking bubbles? I scan the room as if bubbles will jump out at me. Then, as if the fucking bubble gods have shone light on me, my phone vibrates on the counter. Right next to the liquid dish washing bottle, bingo! Bring on the bubbles. I grin back at Keen.

———

I turn on the taps as Keen investigates the bathroom, opening the cabinets and occasionally sitting in them before closing the doors and moving onto the next one. I sit on the toilet lid, watching him with amusement. His body language and gestures are so comical, so like me.

"Keen, the bath is about ready. Wow, can you see all these bubbles, man? I think I might lose you in there." I point to the tub with a grin.

He spins around on his feet, his eyes bugging out at the overflowing bath. His face lights up and he lets out a belly laugh. His little fist shoots into the air. "Yeah. Werhoo!" I grin at his excitement. I did that, and it feels fucking good.

He cocks his head to the side, a thoughtful expression on his little face. "Did you check the water?"

I study his face in question. "What?"

"The water. Jack said you always have to check the water. So you don't get burned." His face all serious and his finger shakes at the bath as if telling it off.

Oh shit! I nearly burned my fucking kid. I shove my hand in the water, then relax when I realize the temperature is fine. My shoulders sag with relief.

Before I understand what's happening, he scrambles to undress, then stands there in front of me with his arms up. Like I know what the fuck he wants.

He sighs at my lack of movement. "I can't climb into the bath. It's too high."

Oh shit, poor little dude. I lift him into the bath, his grin even bigger as he sinks into the mountain of bubbles.

———

When I finally get Keen out of the bath, he's all crinkly and chatting a mile a minute about some television show with a pig on it. Sounds insane if you ask me; this pig wears fucking boots.

As I help him dry off, I scratch my head, realizing we have no clothes for him. I mean, I think there's a change in Will's room, but I don't want to disturb her. I need to prove to her I can handle hard shit like this on my own.

"I'm wondering what you can wear while your mommy is in bed. I don't want to wake her; she had a tough night," I state.

Keen's forehead wrinkles as if he's thinking hard. His little eyes draw together. "I can wear one of your T-shirts?"

I nod, then point to his legs. "I mean, what can you wear instead of your boxers, you know, as pants?" Do they even call little man underwear boxers? I put my hands on my hips. "Come on, I'll call Cal, see what he thinks."

Keen follows behind me, tripping on his towel as I dial Cal.

His voice sounds a million miles away. "Yeah?"

"Cal, what should Keen wear? He doesn't have any boxers and the ones he came in are wet."

"You called me at six thirty a.m. to ask me what to dress your kid in?" I pull the phone away from me slightly, staring at it. His tone fucking stinks.

I put the phone back to my ear. What the fuck is his problem? "Yeah."

"Chloe has been up teething all night. Lily is pissed I came home only a few hours ago. Now you wake me with some dumbass question? Handle your own shit, Con."

He cuts the call, and I stare at the phone, confused. What the hell is his problem? What just happened?

I glance down at Keen and shrug. He stares back up at me with an expression of inquisitiveness about him.

"I'll try Bren." I smile down at him, and he grins back at me and overly nods.

"Bren, dude, minor dilemma. What do I dress Keen in. Will's asleep, and I want to leave her there. Any suggestions?"

"Not got a fucking clue." He cuts the call; I stare at the phone. Seriously, what the fuck is wrong with these people?

I peer at Keen, his eyebrows knitted together. "Don't

worry, little man, I've got more brothers." He nods and gives me a megawatt, encouraging smile.

I pull up Finn's number, taking a deep breath, knowing he isn't aware of my current situation.

"What?" he snaps.

"Finn, purely hypothetical. If you didn't have access to any boxer shorts and needed them, what would you use instead?"

I can hear Finn's steady breathing. Has he fallen back to sleep? "Finn?" I all but bark.

"Go commando."

I shake my head at his suggestion. "No dude, it's for a kid."

His voice comes out confused. "Kid can't do commando?"

"No, no pants. Nothing."

"Jesus." He rummages around, then sighs as though he's thinking about it. "How about a pillowcase? Cut the legs out or something?" See, this is why Finn's my favorite. He's a fucking genius.

"Thanks man." I cut the call with a smile on my face.

Chapter Seven

Con

I sit Keen on the couch, with a long T-shirt covering him. Underneath that is his makeshift boxers. We worked as a team and cut some legs out, then I used tape to secure the waistline. He's now sitting watching the pig program while I watch him. I'm feeling quite impressed with myself, even if I had to ask for Finn's advice; I still achieved it all.

Keen and I work well together, that's for sure. A great team.

"I'm hungry." Keen whimpers while looking at me.

I jump from the couch and go to the kitchen, walking around and opening the cabinets for inspiration. "Okay, little man, you like cereal?" I pull down the Captain Crunch and Beaver Balls.

He nods frantically, then points at me. "No nuts. I'm allergic."

My heart misses a beat. Fuck, I could have killed my kid.

"Are you allergic to anything else?" My heart pounds waiting for his reply.

His eyebrows furrow, then he ticks things off his little fingers. "Peas, lettuce, and those little tree things."

"Little tree things?" I ask, confused.

He nods. "Jack has them at dinner, but I don't. I'm allergic."

I think about what he's saying. "Do you mean broccoli?"

"Yeah, that." He points his finger at me.

Shit, what else is he allergic to? What if I give him the wrong thing and something happens? Fuck, this is some serious shit. I glance at Will's door, biting my lip, unsure of what to do. Then I gaze back at Keen. What the fuck do I do?

He's now sitting on the kitchen stool watching me, waiting for me to feed him.

"How about a drink? You want a drink?" I try to divert his attention from being hungry.

"Yeah, but no apple juice. I'm allergic." He points at me again, with all seriousness.

I open the fridge and see the milk and orange juice. Do I let him have those? Fuck no. I'm not making that mistake.

"How about water? Can you have that?"

He smiles with a tight grin.

Will

Surprisingly, I slept really well. I was so exhausted that after I showered, I literally dropped on the bed and slept through until this morning. Eight thirty, to be precise. I turn over and realize Keen isn't there.

Listening carefully, I hear chuckling from the living area and smile to myself.

I stretch my arms wide before forcing myself out of the bed and freshening up in the en suite bathroom before entering the living area. Con is in the kitchen looking a little stressed. His hair is tussled, his white T-shirt clings to his delectable muscles, and his gray sweatpants hang off his hips. Of course they do.

A throat clears and my eyes dart up to meet his, a smirk on his face. "Morning, beautiful," he practically sings.

I tug awkwardly on my T-shirt, attempting to cover my thighs. Con follows the movement, his blue eyes drinking me in. Slowly, his eyes draw up to meet mine once again, but this time there's fire behind his eyes, and not in a playful, flirty way. No, now he's angry, his jaw clenching.

"Everything okay?" I ask, cautiously moving toward Keen.

"Yep, I had a bath with lots of bubbles!" Keen beams as I kiss him on his forehead.

Thankfully, the tension has been broken by Keen's declaration. "And I'm wearing a pillowcase as pants."

Con winces as I turn to him with raised eyebrows.

He swallows, his eyes darting down, almost looking embarrassed with himself, then he tugs on his hair. "I, erm … didn't want to disturb you, and Keen had an accident. I wanted to fix it myself." He doesn't meet my eyes as he speaks, looking vulnerable. My heart aches a little for him.

"Oh, thank you. For sorting him, I mean. And for not disturbing me. I appreciate it." I try to sound as genuine as possible. Inside, I'm bursting to laugh and hug him all in one.

"Does he pee like that every night? I wasn't sure if he was meant to be in diapers?" Con asks with all seriousness.

Oh jeez, he really has no idea, does he? "No, it's just because he woke up somewhere strange and probably didn't know where the toilet was. Right, buddy?" I peer over at Keen.

Keen points at me. "Yep. And I didn't pee in the bed. I peed when I got out." I stifle a laugh and pull my teeth between my bottom lip as I gingerly stare at Con. He's got his own grin. Our eyes lock, and something passes between us.

Keen drops his feet to the floor and wanders over to the couch, watching *Peppa Pig*.

"So, Keen wanted breakfast, but to be honest, he scared the hell out of me with the whole allergy thing." Con is back to tugging at his hair.

"Oh, shit, his nut allergy. Jesus, with everything that happened yesterday, I completely forgot! Oh my god. You must think I'm such a terrible mom." I start pacing, rubbing my temple, my heart pounding. Shit, I screwed up.

Con rounds the kitchen counter to stop me and pulls me toward him, ducking his head until our eyes meet. "Hey, Will. What the fuck? It's okay, you wouldn't know he'd wake and want food, right? I understand now, and I'll make sure everyone else knows too, okay? No more of this pacing bullshit, it's sorted out. No harm done." He talks with such confidence and power I believe it myself. I breathe out a sigh of relief. No harm done.

Con walks back around the counter and fills the coffee machine.

"I'm sorry. I just had such a rough time with him, and everyone seemed to criticize everything I did. They looked down on me for being a young mother, you know?"

He stops what he's doing, and his eyes dart to meet mine, his tone deepening. "They looked down on you?" His eyebrows furrow.

I meet his eyes, feeling open and vulnerable with the admittance, and chuckle. "Are you kidding? I was a young single mom who didn't have a clue about changing diapers, bottles, colic ..."

"Colic?" Con's eyebrows pull together.

I swing my hand in the air. "Oh, you don't want to know, trust me. Luckily for you, you skipped that stage!"

There's silence between us as the weight of my

words hang there. I hadn't meant it like that, but I'm not taking it back. He deserves some shit for the mess he all but left me in.

Con breaks the tension, slowly working his jaw back and forth. "So, he told me about the nuts, peas, lettuce, broccoli ..."

I hold up my hand. "Wait, he's just allergic to nuts. The others ... He doesn't like them. He's probably trying to get out of eating it or he hasn't quite worked out the difference between like and allergy."

We glance over at Keen. He flicks his gaze between us, his eyes wide. "They make me sick." He shrugs, and there's the answer. Con stifles a grin with his lip trapped between his teeth.

We eat our breakfast at the dining table in virtual silence. Luckily, *Peppa Pig* and Keen's giggles fill the tense atmosphere.

I drop my spoon into my empty bowl and take it over to the sink, avoiding Con's eyes.

He stands and follows me with his bowl in his hand.

Leaning against the countertop, with his voice low and uncertain, he says, "When are we going to talk?"

I avoid his question, not wanting to talk about anything at all. I'm so damn angry with him. I really don't want to talk. "Talk about what?"

He sighs, knowing I'm not making it easy on him, but why the hell should I? "About everything, Will."

"Everything is a pretty broad subject, Con." I'm being a petty bitch, I realize. But again ... Do. Not. Care.

He stands fidgeting on the spot while I tidy the kitchen. How the hell can he make such a mess of serving cereal to three people? "Okay, so do you want to talk about it? What happened between us?"

My spine straightens, my voice low but laced in venom. "You mean the fact you didn't want us? Didn't care to even try to search for me? Search for us?" I scan his eyes for guilt.

His head drops forward. "I didn't try to find you because I was ashamed of how I treated you, Will. Honestly, I thought you'd be better off without me." He gulps at his admission.

"Yeah, well, you should be ashamed. And you're right, we are better off without you, but you came anyway. You came and ruined everything. Every goddamn thing." I practically shout the last few words, and Keen jumps up and peeks over at us, craning his head high like a little meerkat.

"Fuck." Con breathes out slowly, dragging his hand through his hair, licking his lips, contemplating his thoughts and words. He keeps his voice low. "I'm fucking sorry, Will, for everything."

I nod. "You should be, because what you did to us was unforgivable, so don't even think about asking for it." I dry the bowls a little too harshly with the kitchen towel. I'm bubbling inside.

Con nods again, his head still hung low. "I get that I fucked up, Will. I'm not sure how I'm going to show you, both of you, that I can be a better person, but I promise you I'm going to try my best. I swear to you." His words are filled with determination.

Chapter Eight

Con

This morning with Will and Keen went surprisingly well. Apart from Will's dose of reality in the kitchen, it was enjoyable. I can see myself waking up like that regularly. Having Keen around has already given me a sense of purpose, the feeling of someone needing and depending on me and not seeing me for someone who is known as the screwup.

As soon as I can get through to Will how much they can depend on me and maybe even need me, then I can work on getting her to marry me and maybe even have a couple more kids like Keen. God, that would be amazing.

"What the hell are you sitting there grinning about?" Bren's sharp voice breaks my cheerful mood, his nostrils flaring with annoyance. "You realize we're on our way to see Da, right? That you'll probably be walking out of the house with two black eyes and a few broken ribs. If you walk out of there at all?"

I fidget in the passenger seat of his G-Wagon.

Fuck, he's right. My parents will hate me when I drop this clusterfuck on them.

I shuffle in my seat and spin my cap so it's backward. "You said Cal is going to be there, right?" I'm aware I sound childish.

Bren scoffs. "Do you think that sappy fucker can save you?" He raises his eyebrow.

I ignore him and zone out, peering out of the window.

The car slows as we approach the security gates before passing through when the guards are reassured it's us.

Bren parks the car behind Cal's, and I breathe a desperate sound of relief, knowing he's there as moral support. Fuck, am I going to need it.

"You good?" Bren asks while switching off the engine. I shrug. Of course I'm not fucking good. There's a good chance I'll leave here minus a few limbs. My face must pale at my thoughts because Bren's eyebrows knit together before softening slightly. "We got ya. You know that." I dip my head in thanks before taking a deep breath and vacating the car.

Cal gets out of his car and approaches us with a face of determination. "You okay?" I just nod in response.

Cal glances at Bren, and they huddle together with their backs toward me and the house, very fucking inconspicuous. "So, how are we doing this?" Cal asks Bren.

I watch them having their own conversation about my fucking life and deciding how to figure it out for me. Well, fuck that shit. I need to step up and take control. I might be the youngest, dumbest brother, but I've got responsibilities now, and I need to show them I'm capable.

I stride between them, breaking up their little powwow. "I'm doing it. My fuckup. I own it. So I'll deal with it." I throw at them as I stride with purpose toward the house.

I head for the kitchen door and walk straight in.

The smell of homemade bread fills my nostrils. Ma welcomes me in her usual bear hug, her dark hair pulled up in her tight bun, silver glistening in it. She kisses both my cheeks before moving on to my brothers.

I sit at my usual spot at the family table, the last one at the end next to Ma, who sits opposite Da—the king of the table.

Finn normally sits next to me, and if he's not there, his place would be empty, so I'm fucking shocked when Bren drops in his spot instead of his usual one beside Da. Then I'm even more shocked when Cal doesn't take his usual place but sits opposite me next to Ma. I turn toward Bren with confusion. His shoulders widen in a protective stance, his eyes trained on Da coming through the door.

Fuck, they're sat ready for Da to explode, so he'd have to go through one of them to get to me. They're acting as my fucking bodyguards; I don't know whether to be thankful or fucking panicked. My Adam's apple bobs.

Da drops in his seat, his wide body filling it. His posture rigid as normal, on the defense. His famous fighting hands tighten into fists before him. I swallow, not feeling as confident about this showdown anymore.

Ma sits down, wiping her hands on a towel, then she throws it onto her shoulders.

"Why ya sat down there?" Da's voice bellows and fills the room. Ma's eyes dart to mine in worry; she's clearly noted my brothers' protective barrier.

The room falls silent as words evade me.

"Asked ya a feckin' question. Why ya sitting down there?" His stocky finger points at Bren.

Clearing my throat, I sit up straighter. "I … I've something to tell you both." I gulp but continue. "And you're gonna be pissed." I hang my head low in shame and fiddle with my hands on the table.

"Stop fecking stuttering and spit it the fuck out, haven't got all feckin' day!" his intimidating voice barks.

"Okay so——" I clear my throat again and gaze up to catch Cal's eyes. He nods at me in support, and I raise my head to my father. "I've recently discovered I've got a son."

And just like that … he erupts. The chair goes back; his palms slap down on the table, making us all jump. "What? Another fecking kid we know nothin' about? Have you learned nothin from dipshit here?" He waves his hand toward Cal, who rolls his eyes at his nickname.

Not too long ago, poor Cal had to endure this same treatment when he told our parents he was the father of a teenage son, Reece. Luckily for him, he didn't screw up anywhere near as bad as me and managed to keep his O'Connell good looks. He did, however, have to jump through hoops to get out of an arranged marriage in order to marry Reece's mom, Lily.

"How many times do I have to tell ya to wrap ya cocks up!" His hands shake against the table before he lets out a deep breath and rights the chair before begrudgingly sitting back down.

"Well, who the feck is she? She better not be a whore. I ain't having no whore bastard in this house."

I wince at his suggestion. "She isn't a whore, Da." I pull off my cap and brush my hand through my hair, anxiously avoiding the truth. *Rip off the Band-Aid, rip off the Band-Aid. You can do this, Con.* I chant in over and over in my head.

"Con," Bren gently prompts.

I can sense their eyes boring into me like lasers. *Shit.*

I man up, sitting straighter. "It's Will."

"Will?" Ma questions, her knowing eyes meeting mine, and a small smile graces her lips. She and Will always had such a special bond. My ma loved Will and Finn's ex Angel like they were her daughters. I tilt my head to her in confirmation.

"She kept the boy from you?" Da's eyes widen, full of shock. He knew Will and knows that wasn't her type of behavior.

I shake my head in disgust with myself and lick my dry lips. "No. She didn't."

"But you just said you recently found out you had a son. So, which one is it?" Da's voice is laced with annoyance.

I sit bolt upright and straighten my shoulders. "She told me about the baby," I admit weakly.

"Ya talking in fucking riddles. Fucking explain!" Da's finger stubs the table. No doubt seeing through my shit-show of an explanation.

My breath stutters, and I glance out of the corner of my eye at Ma, knowing what I'm about to say will destroy her belief in me. "I'm sorry," I tell her. Tears glisten in my eyes as she gasps.

"What have you done, Connor?" she asks, her voice trembling.

"I ... I ... Shit." Brushing my hand through my hair and staring up to the ceiling, I say, "I asked her to get an abortion." My words come out choked with emotion, but even as I say the words, I realize what I'm saying is wrong, because I didn't ask—I told. "Correction. I told her to get an abortion."

Ma visibly shakes. Her body rigid yet shaking.

Her shuddering hand goes to her mouth as she sobs.

My ma is Catholic through and through and has lost babies herself.

Hell, Bren and Cal can remember her being heavily pregnant but the baby never appearing. We never discussed it with her, but in our hearts, we know Ma must have lost her precious baby. And here I am, demanding for my teenage girlfriend to kill ours. Absolute shame consumes me, my gut roiling with sickness.

Ma doesn't look at me and stares at the table in shock.

"I'm ashamed of what I said and did to Will. If I could take it back ..." I leave my words open and try to peek at Ma. She shakes her head, not wanting to acknowledge the words. Not wanting to look at me, and her gut-wrenching sobs deepen.

Da's quiet, too fucking quiet. "You told her. To get. A feckin' abortion?" Each word poised with venom.

"I did," I admit while staring down at the table, guilt-ridden.

Da's chair goes flying, and he storms around the table at lightning speed.

Bren jumps to his feet, and Cal moves swiftly around the table behind my chair. "Sit the fuck down, Da, come on," Bren practically pleads.

Da's face is red, his eyes bulging, his veins popping, and his fists clench as he launches at me through Bren. "Fucker," Bren grunts when Da's body lands on his.

Da swings in my direction, but I stay seated, prepared to face whatever punishment he sees fit.

His arms flare in all directions as Bren holds him back. "I'll feckin' kill ya. Ya little shite. See how ya like that, eh? She was too good for you, that girl. Too fucking good!"

Don't I know it. I nod agreeing with his words.

Da tries his best to overpower Bren, but it's near on impossible to shift the big fucker.

"Da, you need to calm down. We've more to discuss, and it's serious." Cal hollers over the scrummage.

Ma's sobs break through me, and my hands are shaking. I'd rather my da beat the shit out of me than hear her cry. She sniffles into a small blue teddy bear she keeps in her apron pocket and chants, "Teddy, Teddy" over and over. She always does this when she's hurting or emotional. When we were kids, I asked Cal about it, and he said not to mention it to her. He surmised she'd lost a baby and the pale-blue Teddy she clung to represented the baby. The thought of her losing a baby and me openly pushing Will to kill ours makes me want to vomit.

I don't deserve a family, that's for sure. I deserve no one.

I'm not sure how long it takes Da to settle back into his chair. All I know is my face and body are intact, but my chest fucking hurts, and my heart is ripped open.

How the fuck did Will feel when I asked those things of her?

"You said there was more. More than him wanting to kill his kid?" Da spits the words out like poison, making me wince with the truth behind them.

Cal clears his throat as he sits straighter. "That's right, there's more. Con gave Will the money for the abortion and ended their relationship. When she went to the clinic, they were unable to perform it because she was too far along." Da nods for Cal to continue. I chance a glance at Ma, but her body is tense, and she's staring emptily into space.

"When Will returned home, her father beat her. He was aware of the pregnancy and tried to … tried to kill the baby." Cal swallows thickly. Ma's chair drops back in shock as she stumbles to get up from the table. She walks away, closing the door behind her, but her sobs still echo from the room.

Da stares at me with utter hate in his eyes. His fists clench and unclench. "Ya having it, boy, I'm telling ya. Ya ain't leaving here walking." I nod.

Cal continues talking, ignoring Da's tirade. "Will was dumped at the hospital by her brother. The baby, Keen, barely survived." Da's eyes meet mine when Cal mentions Keen's name. He dips his head sharply with pride, and, if I'm not mistaken, his eyes glisten too.

"He's a fighter, then? Just like my boy," Da confirms.

"Yeah, he is, Da. A little on the small side with the problems Will suffered, but he's perfectly fine," Bren admits.

Da waves in the air. "Plenty of time for him to grow big and strong. It's in the kid's genes. He's an O'Connell." Da's shoulders become broader with pride. "Now, when ya bringing them to see me?"

"There's more ..." Cal grimaces.

"Like feckin' what?" he seethes, his tone changing in an instant.

"Like Will had to hide from her family to protect herself and Keen. Like she married an FBI agent."

"They're divorced," I cut in to lessen the blow.

"A feckin' cop? She married a feckin' cop?" Da's temple throbs, and his nostrils flare like a bull.

Cal ignores his outburst and plows on, swallowing thickly. "She did, and as Con explained, they're now divorced. However, when we met with Will and Jack, her ex, he explained Milo, Will's brother, has put a hit out on her. We're unsure if he's aware of Keen."

Da erupts yet again, and I clench my jaw. How the fuck can you give the guy full details when he constantly blows up like this?! And I'm the childish one.

His face is red, his veins bulging in his forehead.

"This is all your feckin' fault." He points at me, and I nod because he's right.

"Da, enough!" Bren snaps and bangs his fist on the table, causing the silverware to rattle. Like father, like son. I almost roll my eyes at the blatant replica. "Carry on, Cal." He coaxes Cal with a wave of his hand as Da takes his seat again.

"As I was saying. Jack explained the situation to us and agreed it was best for Will and Keen to move in with us while he investigates further."

"Damn feckin' right, they move in with us. We're family," he chimes in.

"As we were leaving the house, a black SUV opened fire on our asses and shot Jack in the chest ..."

"Good, hope the fecker is dead!"

My eyes snap to Da's. He did not just say that. My glare venomous.

He shrugs, unbashful. "He's a cop."

Cal seethes, "That's beside the fucking point. The man stood up and took responsibility for Will and Keen. Protected them and loved them when Con clearly wasn't willing to!"

Wow, Cal's words fucking hurt. I wince at the pain in my chest and fidget in my seat. I scrub my hand through my hair before daring a glance at Cal. His eyes are fixed on mine in a fighting stare-off I'm not prepared for but I turn my head away in defeat.

He's right.

"Wouldn't have gotten shot if he was doing his job properly," Da throws in.

"What-the-fuck-ever. Point being, Milo is a threat, and we need to step carefully with the FBI being involved," Bren states.

"I want him dead. No fecker touches our family. Will's ours, she always has been, always will be." He glares at me. I peer down at my sweaty hands, placing them flat on the table to stop myself from fidgeting.

"You better be stepping the fuck up, ya little shit. You hurt that girl again, and I'll kill ya. Ya hear me?"

I work my head up and down like a fucking puppet. "Yeah, I hear ya, Da. I won't hurt her." I sit straighter and stare at him in the eyes, hoping he can see the truth in them. "I'm going to marry her, give her and Keen what they deserve."

Bren snorts. "She know that?"

Narrowing my eyes, I spin to meet him. "She will soon."

While giving Bren my attention, I hadn't noticed Da getting up from his chair. He moves over toward Cal so he's now opposite me.

His demeanor has changed. He's calmer, almost lighter as he watches Bren's and my exchange. Cal's eyes narrow on Da, unsure of the change in him.

"So, you're gonna marry her, yes?"

I dip my head again in confirmation. "I am."

"Well, ya best crack feckin' on because you ain't gonna be able to jerk yourself off for a while." My eyebrows knit together in confusion.

Before I even see it coming, the bastard stabs me in the fucking hand with a dinner knife.

"Holy fuck, that hurts! Jesus, Da. Did you have to?" My eyes meet his accusingly.

"Shit!" Cal throws out while moving toward my hand … that's fucking stuck to the table!

"Ya lucky it wasn't ya cock, ya little shite. If I didn't think that would hurt Will, it would have been." He smiles smugly, and I know without a doubt he'd do it too.

Thank fuck for Will.

Da moves back to his chair and pulls a cigar out of his shirt pocket, lighting it. "Now, about this Milo fucker. Kill him." His pupils dilate, and his grin turns sinister.

Chapter Nine

Will

This morning, Cal called to say Jack was stable in the hospital and being guarded by a couple of trusted colleagues. To say I was relieved is an understatement. Jack has been an incredible part Keen's and my life. I don't honestly know what we would do without him.

Keen and I spend the afternoon in Con's apartment while he's gone to explain our situation to his parents. A flutter turns my stomach when I imagine what Con will be up against at his parents' house. I quickly shut that emotion down. *He deserves it.*

I make myself at home. Luckily, Cal's wife, Lily, had the forward thought to send us a grocery order so I could stock the cupboards and fridge. I've never been so grateful for some fresh produce. How Con survives, I'll never understand, but judging by the state of the apartment when we arrived, I probably don't want to know either.

I also may have snooped a little to keep myself busy,

but when I opened Con's bedroom door and his familiar masculine scent hit me, I rushed to close it. I couldn't face going in there, being drawn in again. No, I need to keep my defenses up and keep him at a safe distance. There's Keen to consider this time around, and there's no way in hell is he going to hurt my son.

The elevator pings, and Con strides into the room, his aura surrounding me and stilling my breath. How can he still have this effect on me?

His eyes dart to mine before dipping to my chest, my tight camisole top leaving nothing to the imagination. I'm without a bra, due to the fact the only one in my possession is in the washer. My nipples pebble under his scrutiny. He licks his lips, and I'm sure he's not even aware he's doing it, and my breath hitches in response.

His heady voice laced with need. "Will."

"Mmm?" I snap my eyes up to meet his, trying to ignore that tongue, those lips. God, those lips.

"Miss me?" He grins.

I shrug. "Not really."

How can I not miss him when he's everywhere in this apartment, yet nowhere at all?

He walks toward me with purpose. "I missed you." He scans my face. "And Keen. Where is my little dude, anyway?" His eyes dart around the apartment.

I nod toward the corridor leading to the bedrooms. "He's putting some toys away. Lily sent some over for him."

Con scrubs a poorly bandaged hand through his hair, with blood seeping through it, and winces. "Yeah, he's going to need his own room, isn't he?"

"What happened to your hand?" I ask while pulling his wrist toward me.

He exhales deeply. "Da fucking stabbed me. Prick." He spits the latter out with hate.

My eyebrows shoot up. "Your Da did it?"

"Yeah, said I was lucky it wasn't my cock." He chuckles. Actually freaking chuckles.

I shake my head. "You're insane, the both of you." I walk him into the kitchen and unwrap his hand. "Why would he do that?" I ask as I reach for the first aid kit above the oven.

My top lifts as I stand on my tiptoes to reach for it. Before my feet touch the ground, a soft hand snakes around my waist. Con pulls me to him so my back is against his front. His breath sends goose bumps erupting over my body, and he moves his mouth to my ear. "You want to know why he stabbed me?"

My words clog in my throat, so I nod, those pesky words evading me.

I'm consumed with Con's hand splayed across my stomach, under my top, his nose at my neck, breathing me in, and his hardness pushing against my back.

"I told him I was going to marry you."

Like a douse of cold water over me, I bristle at his words, my spine rigid. All thoughts consuming me are gone in an instant. "Don't pull away from me, Will. You're mine. This is happening." His lips tease my neck, and I shake my head. He tightens his hand on me and pulls me to him. Closer. Tighter. "I'm never letting you leave, Will." His gentle but confident voice pisses me off.

I shake my head again. "You don't own me, Con."

He chuckles in my ear. "No, maybe not yet. But you own me." He rubs his cock against my ass for emphasis.

I gasp at the sensation. "You always have, Will. I was

just too dumb to realize it. It's always been you." I close my eyes at his admission, determined not to cry. I can't.

When I don't react, he pushes my boundaries further, goading me for a reaction. The right reaction. "I love you. Do you hear me?" My heart skips, and I break at his words. My knees give way, and I can't stop the wail that leaves my mouth.

"Shhh, baby. I've got you," he coos while holding me up. His fingers dig into my hips. "I've got you." Kissing my hair he says, "I'm all in." I bend over, quietly sobbing at his words and promises. He holds me close, letting me cry.

How many times I've wanted to hear those words, feel this support. So many times. I stifle my emotions by biting my lip.

"Mommy, I did a poop!" Keen proudly shouts from the bathroom, breaking our moment. I've never been more grateful for hearing those poop words declared in my entire life.

Con chuckles to himself. "I got this." He gently releases me and kisses the back of my head.

I clear my throat and avoid his eyes. "Don't forget to wipe his tush."

Con stops on the spot and spins round, a blank expression on his face. "Huh?"

"His butt. He needs it wiped." I gesture with my hand, swiping up.

"He doesn't do that?" I stare up at Con, his handsome face looking all sorts of unsure.

"No, Con, believe me, he tries. Be grateful he's shouting he's pooped from inside the bathroom and not from another room."

Con grimaces, then nods and moves on toward the

bathroom. I listen, hoping to hear what their hushed conversation is about but can't make it out. I stifle a small giggle at the thought of Connor trying to wipe a very independent but not competent Keen.

———

Con ended up bathing Keen while I started on dinner; he said something about it being easier to wash the shit away than wipe it.

I made spaghetti with a side salad, and Con grins from ear to ear when he scrapes the last of his meal into his mouth. "Fuck, you can cook."

My eyes go wide, then dart to Keen, whose eyes are bugging out. "Oh, shit. I'm sorry. Keen don't say that word, okay?" I glare in his direction. I mean, is he serious? Like shit is okay to say?

"I don't. I'm not a naughty boy." He sits proudly in his chair, wearing a smug little smile on his face which makes him appear even more like Con, with his bright-blue eyes mirroring his father's.

Con's shock soon turns into something more playful as he gazes at me. "Am I a naughty boy, Will?"

My eyebrows rise. Is he serious? Yep, that sly smile tells me he is. I sharpen my tone. "Yep, he's very naughty, Keen. Don't repeat the naughty words." I decide not to play Con's game as I eyeball him.

"Are you naughty, Will?" Con grins, undeterred.

I peek at Keen, his eyes darting between mine and Con's, trying to figure out if either of us is naughty.

"Nope, can't say that I am." I give him a sarcastic, tight smile back.

"Pretty sure you are." With childlike glee in his eyes, a smile encompasses his face.

I roll my eyes at him. "Nope. Definitely a good girl."

Con watches me and brushes his hand over his jaw. "Mmm, I'm not so sure."

The elevator pings, causing all our eyes to dart toward the door.

In walks a tall platinum blonde, in a freaking trench coat and high heels.

Red lips, bright-red nails, red heels. "Hey, handsome," she purrs with a sultry wave.

My mouth drops open, and Con jumps up from his chair so fast it hits the floor. He runs toward her and she opens her coat to reveal a red bra and panties. "Oh, fuck! Cher, don't open the fucking coat." Yeah, a little too late on that, Con.

I watch in complete shock as Cher opens the coat wider before trailing her nails down Con's chest. "I want to play," she pouts with her thick fake lips. She seems oblivious to the family at the table.

My stomach churns.

"Can I play too?" Keen calls as he stands on his chair for a better view.

Oh god, no! "What the hell, Con?" I screech over my shoulder as I stand and block Keen's view.

"Fuck. Outside. Get the fuck outside," he snaps at her while I coax Keen to bed with a cookie and promise of a visit to the park tomorrow.

I glance at the door and realize they've both gone through it. My shoulders sagging, I pick Keen up and march him to our room.

My heart is full of annoyance and, yeah, as much as I hate to admit it, disappointment too.

Con

Shit. I fucked up … again.

Cher comes by twice a week for our little rendezvous. I'd completely forgotten about her. I mean, why the fuck would I even think about her when I've got Will consuming every second of my mind?

By the time I get her out the fucking door and explain I'm not interested anymore, I felt fucking sick at the thought of letting Will down again. What the fuck must she think of me? Cher might have been an okay fuck, but that's all she ever was, and she was fine with it.

I message Oscar and ask him to change the security details so we have no more unexpected guests. I sure as hell don't need any of the guys who I party with showing up here.

I'm walking back into the apartment, ready to apologize, but when I see Will in a long baggy T-shirt, my anger morphs. It's not just any baggy shirt, it's a man's T-shirt. And it's not fucking mine. My jaw clenches so tight my fucking teeth hurt.

Will's soft voice cuts through my tension. "I put Keen to bed. He was exhausted."

I nod, but I'm pissed she put him to bed without me.

After storming to my bedroom, I rummage through my drawers. If she wants something to wear, I'll fucking give it to her.

I rage through the apartment to where Will is wiping the kitchen surfaces. My face must scream pissed. My temples throb, my hands are clenched, and my nostrils are flared.

"What the hell are you wearing?" I spit.

Will turns to face me, her face a picture of shock. She looks down at herself, then back up at me, confused.

"You're wearing another man's shirt in my apartment," I state.

Her eyebrows rise, then her expression changes as she chokes slightly before giving me lip. "You have got to be fucking kidding me, Con! I've just had a front-row seat of some pumped-up strip show, and you're lecturing me on what I'm wearing?" Her chest rises as she points at the door.

I shrug off her comment. "You have nothing to worry about where Cher's concerned. She doesn't matter. She means nothing to me."

If I thought that would pacify her, I was fucking wrong. Apparently, very wrong.

Her nostrils flare. "Nothing to worry about? What the hell are you talking about? I don't give a shit who you screw. Just don't flaunt her in front of me and Keen. We deserve respect, Con." Her voice softens at the end, enraging me more. She doesn't care? My heart races wildly. Doesn't care?

I scoff. "Take the fucking shirt off, Will!" I spit.

Her chin rises. "No."

My chest heaves as I stare into her defiant eyes. They're gleaming with a dare.

I step toward her and hold her shirt by the scruff of the neck. I twist my face as I grip the shirt in my fists. A roar erupts from me and I rip the shirt from her body. It hangs loosely on both sides of her body. Her arms just hang beside her, her lips parted beautifully. Fuck, she's gorgeous.

I seethe with barely restrained rage as I take in her gorgeous body. She trembles under my gaze. Her tits hanging free, her perfect pink nipples on display, begging to be sucked. I lick my lips.

Her small black lace panties barely cover her pussy. *Fuck.* I gulp thickly.

I work my eyes back up to her face. My eyes meet hers, and she can't mask the want in them, the need, but she also can't mask the hurt still shining through.

I can't fucking stand it.

"Turn the fuck around!" I spit. She doesn't move, just looks at me in a trancelike state. "Turn, Will. Fucking turn," I demand, spinning my finger in a motion I expect her to understand.

She slowly turns, but my impatience takes over, so I spin her around and push her hands onto the countertop.

"Co ... Con?"

"Shut up. Shut the fuck up. I need this." I bite into my lip.

She goes still as I yank her panties down. "Did you love him, Will? Did you love your fucking husband?" I snipe the words out with bitterness.

"Ye ... yes, of course."

I nod even though she can't see me. My heart pounds violently against my chest with her admittance. "I never felt a goddamn thing for any of them. Not one. Do you hear me? You. Fucking. Own. Me!" I'm so beyond pissed at her. For the shirt, for her loving someone else, for hating me. I just want her to want me, to need me. Like I need her.

I roughly tug my buttons down my jeans. If I could rip them off me, I would. My dripping cock springs free, hitting my stomach. The soreness from not wearing boxers and my cock rubbing against my jeans adds to my heightened, aggressive state. She'll fucking pay for causing that. I grind my teeth when Will tries to turn her body around.

I roughly push the middle of her back down and kick her legs farther apart. Gripping my cock with fury, I ram it into her, not caring if she's ready. Not caring if she wants me as much as I want her. I know she wants me. She'd have voiced it if not.

Air rushes from her chest at the sudden intrusion. I smirk and grip her hips as she wiggles her ass from side to side to accommodate me.

"Fucking take it!" I grit out.

Her breathy moans urge me on. "Ah. Oh god, Con." Her hands clench the countertop tighter.

"Fucking standing here, dressed like this." I pound into her, taking her to her tiptoes. "In another man's shirt? You're fucking mine. Do you understand me?" I grip her roughly, no doubt leaving bruises as my cock thrusts into her relentlessly. "Say you fucking understand." Her pussy clenches around my cock at my words.

"Fucking. Say. It!"

Her breath ragged. "Yours. I'm yours."

My body eases at her words, my words coming out softer this time. "Yeah, you are. You're mine." I nip at her neck, then kiss away the bite.

Her pussy clutches me like a vise. I move my uninjured hand to her tit and grasp the cushioned breast forcefully, tweaking her nipple. Fuck, it feels good. My mouth waters for them, my balls tighten at the thought. I've never felt the need to fuck someone so much, so hard, so desperately.

"Will, I'm close, baby. I'm fucking close." I clench myself to try and tame my cock.

I gaze down at our combined bodies. My body pounding against her sweet ass. Ramming in and out of her pussy.

"Fuck, you're still tight. So tight." My mouth falls lax from pleasure.

"Oh, fuck, Con. Like that." My naughty girl loves her tits being squeezed. "Yes. Oh, I'm going to …" Her words end as she drops her head forward, and her pussy grips me with intensity.

I throw my head back with the force of my orgasm, my cum flooding her pussy with vigor.

"Fuck yes, take it, Will. Take it all."

Her hands turn to fists on the counter as our orgasms consume us. I push one final time, ensuring my cum is as far in as possible. She collapses on the counter with such force she winces, and I fall into her.

We pant in unison, our bodies laced with sweat.

I straighten as I hold her hips and gently stand her back upright. My cock slips from her, and my cum flows down her thighs. I watch in awe as it covers her, marking her, then use my bad hand to push the cum back into her swollen pussy. The thought of owning her inside and out possesses me.

"You ... you didn't use a condom." I still at her words. She turns her head over her shoulder to stare at me with desperation evident in her eyes.

My shoulders tense once again. "I'm clean, Will. I've never ..." I leave the words hanging there as I wave my hand in her pussy's direction.

She nods with uncertainty. A vulnerable look in her eyes as she turns and tries to cover herself with the remains of the shirt. "I'm on birth control." She drops her head. Is she meaning to reassure me? What the fuck? Does she not get it? Does she not understand? My eyebrows pull together; how can she not understand my intentions?

I shrug. "Stop taking it."

She sucks in a dramatic breath before she throws her head back and mock laughs. Is she for real right now?

"Jesus, Con, you've had us here for two days!" She all but shouts, her tone laced with condescension.

I shake my head, licking my lips. "Doesn't matter. You're not leaving."

She lets out an exaggerated exhale before holding her hand up and shaking her head. "I can't deal with this shit right now. I'm going to bed." And with that, she turns and walks away, leaving me standing there with a throbbing hand, a semi, and my T-shirt.

Chapter Ten

Will

I just showered and am still in a postsex daze from the night before, standing in front of the mirror. Tilting my head from side to side, I survey the bruises on my hips left by the aggressive sex with Con yesterday.

I clench my thighs at the reminder. My pussy still swollen and, surprisingly, still needy.

When I woke again this morning, Keen was already awake. Con and he were chatting away together and giggling. It's become a morning routine, a routine that melts my heart. Keen wakes early, and Con sits watching *Peppa Pig* with him until I get up. Then we all have breakfast together like a family.

I tug on a camisole top and pull on a pair of leggings. I'm running dangerously short on clothes with very few selections available. That's definitely something I need to resolve. I sigh, pull my hair up into a messy bun, and head out to the living room.

My footing wavers as I approach the living area. Con is lying bare chested on the couch with Keen sitting on his stomach happily munching on a cookie, his cute face coated in crumbs.

Con's abs are on full display, his wavy hair wet, probably from a shower. He lies in gray sweatpants with an arm tucked behind his head, looking every bit the sexy man he is. I lick my lips, imagining running my tongue down his toned body. Keen's giggle breaks my stare.

"Morning," I say as I approach Keen, then bend down and kiss his messy curls. As I do, Con's hand brushes up the back of my thigh and pulls me closer to them. I reluctantly meet his eyes, and he smiles softly, his blue eyes flash with vulnerability, unsure of himself and my reaction. His gentle touch and brushing motion giving me goose bumps, so I have to push away the memories of his hands roaming desperately over my body.

I wipe the crumbs from Keen's cheeks and smile. My little monster is covered.

"Morning, Mommy, I'm hungry," he says, struggling to watch me and not *Peppa Pig*.

I roll my eyes. "You're always hungry, little man."

I go to move away, but Con's hand tightens, and his eyes are transfixed on my braless breasts. Typical. I internally roll my eyes.

"I need to get some new clothes. I'm a little limited." Grimacing, I try to explain, a little embarrassed at the display.

Con clears his throat. "I don't know. I think I like you limited." He chuckles with a smirk, and I playfully swat his hand away from my thigh and move toward the kitchen.

After filling the coffee machine, I start working on breakfast.

Con leaves Keen on the couch and comes into the kitchen, leaning on the countertop, and watching me move around the kitchen. His broad shoulders are on full display, with his elbows on the counter. I try not to pay attention to the way my body is craving his.

"You can order some clothes online if you want?" he suggests.

"I have clothes at home," I state without turning to face him.

He sighs. "Don't be difficult, Will. Just order some new shit, okay?"

He's right. It wouldn't be wise to go home for clothes. I sigh and drop my head. "Sure."

I decide to change the subject to something a little lighter. "I promised Keen I'd take him to a park today."

Con's body tightens. "That's not a good idea. Not until I speak to Bren, anyway. Besides, I made plans for us today."

I turn sharply, irritated. "Plans?"

He looks unsure of his words and brushes a hand through his wavy locks. "Yeah. Lily and Cal invited us over. I thought it would be nice for you to meet Lily so you have a friend here. Then Keen could have a play-date, meet Reece and Chloe? They have a garden full of stuff, like a pirate ship and shit." His words come out fast and persuasive.

I soften at his thoughtfulness. I quite like the idea. It'll be nice to meet Con's niece and nephew; he's told me so much about them and Cal speaks about them with such pride it'll be nice to finally put faces to their names.

"Great." I smile at him. "Keen, come on little man, breakfast!" I call over Con's shoulder, and his grin broadens at my enthusiasm.

Chapter Eleven

Will

We pull into Cal and Lily's gated community. Con had explained they previously lived in one of their apartments, but when Lily found out she was pregnant, Cal surprised her with a family home. And wow, did he do good.

The mansion is nestled behind manned gates, but being surrounded by trees, they're not visible, giving the illusion of privacy.

The car rolls along the cobbled driveway. I stare out of the window in awe, imagining Keen climbing the trees.

"You like it?" Con asks, watching me closely as the SUV slows while approaching the mansion.

I turn to meet his eyes. "What's not to like? It's beautiful."

He grins at my remark. "Good. I was hoping you'd say that." He smiles.

What the hell does that mean?

I watch Con a little closer, searching for answers, but all I see is an excited manchild. Correction, a hot, excited manchild. He's wearing a backward baseball cap, with curls poking through, a white tight T-shirt that stretches over his muscular shoulders, and jeans which look painted on with how the shape of his thighs can be made out in the denim. He eyes me again before giving me a knowing wink, causing my eyes to roll at his cockiness.

We exit the car, and Con expertly unstraps Keen. "Come on, dude, time to go meet some new friends." His voice is laced with enthusiasm.

"No!" Keen stomps. My poor little man is nervous, so he tugs his hair a little, then sucks his thumb, unsettled and unsure how to act. He then comes running around to me and clings to my legs for reassurance.

Con watches him with a look of pain on his face. His Adam's apple bobs, no doubt hurt by Keen's actions. Yeah, he needs to get used to little strops and tantrums.

I swallow my pride and decide to take pity on Con and bend down to Keen. "Keen, Con has all sorts of fun things planned today. He said that little Chloe has a jungle gym and a pirate ship. Would you like to see it?"

Keen nods.

Out of the corner of my eye, I see Con visibly relax. I glance up at him, and he mouths an appreciative *Thank you*. I offer him a small, tentative smile.

We turn to walk up the steps toward the front door, and Con reaches for my hand, but I pull away. "Fuck, I'm sorry, Will. I can't stop myself." He doesn't meet my eyes as he tries to explain.

The funny thing is, I get it. I understand how natural it is to hold him. That's why I'm trying to stay closed off with him. I can't step over the line and give myself to him again, not yet. Maybe not ever.

"You said a naughty!" Keen is quick to chastise, forgetting he's nervous.

Con and I eye one another, probably thinking the same thing. I stifle a laugh, clamping my teeth over my bottom lip.

Con's hand brushes against the small of my back as he leads us through the front door, his breath on my ear as he whispers, "I'm rock hard imagining me stuffing that pretty mouth of yours with my cock, Will."

I choke. Literally choke on my spit. What the hell?! My eyes bug out as I spin to see his grinning face, his gleaming teeth on full display. Proud of his confession, he then licks his lips seductively. I dart my eyes back down to Keen; he's completely unaware, taking in the room.

A throat clears in the hallway. "Finished with the games, Connor?" Cal's stern voice cuts through the sexual tension. He stands in navy shorts and a white T-shirt, looking completely unlike his usual businessman self.

Con chuckles. "Actually, no, I haven't even started." I elbow him in his stomach, earning an "Ouch."

Before I can move forward to greet Cal, I hear pattering feet, and in comes a very flustered-looking brunette. She's petite, with her hair tied into a messy ponytail, and she's wearing an off-the-shoulder shirt and ripped jeans. Lily pushes past Cal and virtually flings herself at me. "Hi, I'm Lily. It's sooo good to meet you. Oh my God, wow! You are a mini-Con aren't you?" she declares, staring down at Keen. Then, realizing her mistake, she clamps her hand over her mouth. "Oh my

God. I'm so sorry. Oh God!" Her face is a picture of mortification at her mistake.

I take her panicking hand. "It's fine. He's a little out of sorts, and I'm not sure he'd put it together anyway," I say to reassure her.

Lily nods. "Okay. Okay. So come on, follow me." She takes my hand and literally pulls me down the corridor, guiding me outside.

I chance a glance at Con over my shoulder. He's still standing in the doorway with an anxious-looking Keen.

Lily waves her hand around. "Oh, don't worry about them. I've given Cal strict instructions to leave us the hell alone and amuse the kids with Con." I laugh at her declaration. "Honestly, it's so good to have another female in the family." She babbles while leading us outside.

She shows us to a patio area overlooking a generous, enclosed pool that looks like a lagoon. Beyond that is a children's play area, complete with a jungle gym and wooden pirate ship. I take it all in while Lily pulls out her seat, gesturing to the surrounding chairs, and I move to sit opposite her.

"Erm, how old is Reece?" I ask, confused. I thought I already knew the answer.

Lily bursts into laughter. "I know, right? He's fifteen now. Oh, don't for one minute think any of this is for him!" She waves her hand at the play area. "Nope, that's all for Chloe! You know, our nine-month-old daughter!" She rolls her eyes at my wide-eyed expression. "Oh, I completely agree. Cal is absolutely insane; I mean, by the time she can play on it. She'll need a new one." She sighs dramatically while dropping into her seat.

"Wow, I thought Con was the O'Connell manchild."

Lily beams at me. "I think they all are. Secretly, anyway." She winks.

She offers me a drink from the selection of slush cocktails she has on the table. She's really gone to town and even made a fruit platter. I smile as she pours me an orange cocktail, complete with fancy decoration. "This, this is all Cal," she explains, motioning toward the fruit and cocktails. "I have to stick with juice." She sighs, pouring herself a fruit juice. "I'm still breastfeeding. Well, weaning anyway."

"Well, he's done great." I smile back.

"He has, hasn't he?!" She smiles dreamily.

"So, where's Reece?" I ask, searching around the grounds.

"Oh, I'm so sorry. He's at Oscar's. I swear those two are thick as thieves. They're constantly trying to outsmart one another." She shakes her head while smiling. Her entire personality is infectious. "You'll meet him at the family meal on Sunday, of course," she declares.

My hand stops before the drink reaches my mouth. "Meal?"

"Yeah, we have to attend every week." She grimaces.

I forgot about the family meal. I used to look forward to them, but after Brennan stabbed Con with a knife, I'm a little apprehensive about taking Keen. He's not used to Brennan's whole brash demeanor. Keen's timid, sometimes a little too timid.

"Don't worry, we'll all be there to support you. And apparently, Brennan can't wait to see you and meet Keen. Cyn is bursting at the seams, of course." Lily pats my hand in support.

"Thanks. It's just a lot to take in." I swallow harshly.

Lily nods in understanding. "So … how's it going with Con?"

I blow out a breath. "Fine. I mean, we get on. We always have. It's just I wasn't prepared to see him again, let alone have him back in my life with such bold determination." I admit on a fake chuckle.

Lily watches me closely, seeing through my facade. "Yeah, Cal explained what happened. I'm so sorry you had to go through that, Will. I understand it's none of my business, and it's the only thing I'm going to say, but Cal has always said Con has never been the same since you left. He's always said his heart was broken."

I scoff at her words. *His* heart was broken?

"I hope with the way he treated you, you're making him pay, though?" She raises her eyebrow in jest. And just like that, my anger dissipates.

———

Loud giggling interrupts our easy conversation, and Cal strides over with a beautiful baby girl in his arms, her pretty, frilly pink dress on display and her chubby hands pushed into Cal's mouth as she babbles away. She's utterly adorable, with untamed brown curls and a little pink bow in the front.

"She wanted to see Mommy before going to play," Cal explains while lowering Chloe onto Lily's lap.

"She was having nap time," Keen informs me, his smile wide.

"She was?"

Keen nods. His head is now covered in Con's baseball cap, and I wonder to myself if he had to give it to him to coax him from the front door.

"Oh, you're such a beautiful girl, Chloe," I tell her as Lily bounces her on her knee. Chloe reaches out for me, and Lily nods for me to take her.

I lift her into my lap, instantly loving the reminder of having the weight of a baby on me. A smile graces my face as I snuggle into her scent. Chloe pushes her fist into her mouth, babbling away.

"She's trying to eat her hand, Mommy!" Keen giggles as he kneels before her, causing us all to laugh at their cute interaction. "She's a silly girl, aren't you, Chloe?" he coos.

I smile to myself, then lift my head to find Cons' eyes on me, drilling into me like laser beams.

When he realizes I'm watching him, he swallows thickly, then quickly glances away.

"Come on, little princess, let's get you on that swing," Cal declares while lifting Chloe from my arms.

Keen fist pumps the air and follows suit, with Con trailing behind them.

Once they're out of earshot, Lily turns to me. "Sooo, Con looked like he was about ready to knock you up just then."

I splutter on my drink and act innocent. "He did?"

"Mm-hm. He looked like he was ready to take you right out here. His eyes never left you and Chloe. I hope you're on birth control, Will. In fact, scrap that, make sure you're on birth control and use condoms," she says while pointing a finger at me. "Cal knocked me up while I was on the pill." She exhales for effect.

My eyes bug out. "No way?!"

"I know, right?! What are the chances?"

"Well, there will be no pitter patter of tiny feet from me," I say, while raising my chin.

"Yeah, that's what I said." She laughs.

We chat for a while about kids, Cal's obsession with creating the perfect family environment, and how great a dad he is to his children and how they came to be together. Lily appears as completely and utterly in love with Cal as he is with her, and I can't help the small pang of jealousy at their beautiful family life.

"So, Will, you were married previously? And Cal says you're good friends with your ex? That's pretty impressive." A genuine smile graces Lily's lips.

"Yes. Jack and I met when I was at a hostel for single mothers needing help. He was volunteering with legal advice, that sort of thing. Anyway, he helped a lot when I explained about my circumstances." I shuffle from side to side, slightly uncomfortable sharing my story, but I continue with determination. "So, we basically got close. He was great and patient with Keen, amazingly supportive, actually. We grew close quickly. Before I knew it, we set up a family home and were married."

Lily listens intently, and her eyebrows furrow. "So, what went wrong?"

I think about her question. "Nothing per se. I just think we both wanted a perfect family, but in fact, we were better off as just friends."

Lily stares at me a little shocked, so I decide to elaborate a little deeper. "Jack has a hero persona. He had a high school romance that ended through the girl suffering from abuse within her family. Anyway, it was for those reasons he joined the FBI and volunteers at hostels. When we got together, I think we needed each other as a crutch? Does that make sense?"

Lily nods softly. "I understand. You supported one

another when you needed it. Your relationship was based on the support for one another."

"Exactly. Don't get me wrong, I love him. I'll always love him. But it's not the same kind of love." Not the same love I have for Con is what I don't say, and I catch him tickling a giggling Keen on the grass. My heart instantly beats fast, but I swallow away the emotion their interaction brings.

As if reading between the lines, Lily grins. She subtly changes the subject when I school my expression. "Keen never called Jack dad?" she asks, but it's more of a statement.

"No. Neither Jack nor I encouraged him. It's almost like we both knew that Jack wasn't in it for the long term. We actually both openly corrected him." I wince at the memory.

"You did right, Will. You're doing right." I meet Lily's eyes, and they're filled with love and admiration; she will be such a great friend; I can see the sincerity in her eyes. I'm so lucky to have met her and be welcomed as part of the family once again.

Con

Being with Will and Keen at Cal's today has been incredible. How the fuck anyone can live their lives without their own family is beyond me.

No sooner than I think that thought do I have the jolt of reality that, that is exactly what I was doing. I was living my life without my family; the thought instantly sickens me. The pain returns to my chest, clogging my throat.

Will throws her head back, laughing at something Lily is saying, and the expression on her gorgeous face gives me an instant boner.

Not great when my three-year-old kid insists on running into me every three damn seconds, knocking the fuck out of my dick and balls.

I wince as Keen rebounds off me to climb the pirate ladder for the hundredth time. His energy is unreal. He reminds me of my brother, Keenan. My mouth goes dry, and I push the sadness aside.

Glancing back at Will, I swallow thickly. Her beautiful brown locks hang down her back, and her light-blue summer dress exposes her slender shoulders. The neck-line of the dress dips down to her tits, which are fortu-nately covered by a new bra. Otherwise, I'm pretty sure those edible nipples would be on full display too. Fuck yeah. I scrub a hand down my face with a painful groan. I'm not sure this is the distraction I need right now.

I scrutinize her a little more. She's so fucking beautiful it hurts. I will be a better man for her, for Keen, and my brother.

My eyes follow her chest as she laughs and her tits bounce. Fuck, I need to touch them, mark them.

I was pretty fucking glad when a bundle of clothes was delivered to us this morning. Now Will can leave the house with underwear on, and no fuckers can see her sexy body on full display. Even if we are only going to my brothers', I still don't want him looking at her like that. No, I'd knock the pricks out for even daring to peek.

"What are you looking so pissed about?" Cal asks while standing by the picnic blanket he laid down for Chloe.

I glance down at my hard dick and lift my T-shirt to show him.

His face morphs into utter revulsion, his eyes bugging out. "Jesus, Con! Seriously? Around the kids?" he scowls.

"I can't fucking help it. It won't go down!" I spit back in equal, measured disgust.

Cal's eyes search around, and he waves his hands around his property, his voice turning lighter. "Think fucking trees, bushes, or something like that." He breathes out sharply.

I choke. "Bushes? Now you've got me thinking of

Will's lack of bush. And that isn't fucking helping." I shake my head. "No. You gotta help me out, man."

Cal's head spins toward me, his wide eyes drawing in. He lowers his tone dangerously. "Help you out how? What the fuck are you talking about?" He swallows harsh. His words bitter.

I chuckle at his panic riddled voice. "I need some alone time with Will." Nodding in her direction with hopeful eyes, I watch for Cal's reaction.

Cal's shoulders relax before tightening again. "Absolutely not," he all but spits.

"Fuck, man, come on. Do you really want me to sit at the dinner table eating lunch with Lily around and my rock-hard dick?"

His lips tighten into a firm line with the thought, his fists flaring at the side of him.

"Fucking fine," he spits. "You can have the garage. Twenty minutes. Tops." He presses something on his phone, and I can only assume he's switching the cameras off in the garage.

"The garage? Can you not do better than that? Like a bed? Fuck, Cal, you've got like eight rooms here." I gesture to the monstrosity he calls a home. Selfish prick can't even spare a bed?

"No, Con, you're not coming over here for a fuck fest. You either use the garage or sit in tight jeans." He triumphantly grins.

"Fine," I snap out, annoyed at the moody fucker. If I sit in front of Will with her delectable body on display, I'm liable to cream my jeans.

Garage it is.

Will

"Will, follow me. I want to show you something!" Con shouts as he walks across the manicured gardens, heading to the garage and looking like a man on a mission.

I lift my eyes over my drink and stare at Lily for guidance, and she just shrugs. Glancing over at Cal with the kids in the play area, he has an unamused expression on his face. His hands are on his hips, watching Con with a disgruntled look in his eyes.

"Will!" Con barks out at me.

I roll my eyes at his impatience. "Excuse me, Lily, I'm sure I'll be back in a few minutes." Pushing my chair away, I make my way over to the garage on the far side of the property. I follow with uncertainty through the door that Con walked through a few moments ago.

Apprehensively, I walk into the dimly lit garage, and my eyes attempt to adjust to the poor lighting. Before I have a chance to call out for Con, I feel his presence behind me. The hairs on the back of my neck stand up in excitement.

His breath trickles down my neck as his hands gently stroke over my hips. He pushes himself into me. "Fuck, I need you, Will. So fucking bad." He kisses down my neck and massage my hips before creeping up my dress. "I need you so bad I'm going to fucking explode." His voice is already ragged with need.

"Con," I pant out.

"Fuck yeah, say my name again." His lips tug on the sensitive skin of my neck. Soft, exploring lips trail kisses, and he tugs and sucks along my neckline and shoulders.

"You smell so fucking good, Will." He breathes in my scent.

His hands move over my thighs, caressing and massaging, causing wetness to pool between my legs.

He pants out his words. "Say you want me. Say you want me as much as I want you."

I say nothing, scared to admit the truth. He nuzzles into my throat and neck, then bites my upper shoulder. "Say it." His voice is firm and demanding, but I shake my head in defiance.

"You fuck up my head, Will. I can't think straight with you around me. I just need to be inside you all the time." He grits the words out as though they pain him. "Making you mine all the time. Owning you all the time. Because I do own you, Will. Every bit of you."

"Your mind." He spins me around and kisses my forehead.

"Your tits." He bends down and kisses my tits one by one. My nipples pebble in response.

"Your pussy." I suck in a breath as he lowers to his knees. Moving my dress aside, he kisses me over the top of my panties before he spins me again so I'm facing the wall.

"Your ass." He dips back under my dress and kisses both ass cheeks before caressing them. His damaged hand long forgotten.

"Take off your dress, Will," he commands.

I hesitate for a moment too long, and he growls, then sharply slaps my ass. "Do it!"

I jump at his gruffness and tug my sundress over my head, letting it to pool to the garage floor. "Now put your hands on the wall."

I do as I'm told, my palms hitting the wall.

Con tugs my panties to my knees. His jean buttons pop open. I expect his cock to push into me at any second, but when I feel his breath in the crook of my ass, I gaze over my shoulder. And holy hell, the sight has me almost coming undone on the spot.

Con is on his knees with his engorged cock in hand, stroking himself while licking his lips in anticipation. Our eyes meet, and he smiles a cocky grin. He lunges forward, and with the other hand, he parts one ass cheek and pushes his face into me. His warm breath and wet tongue give me sensation overload as he licks around my ass. Con's tongue pushes in for deeper access. His groans rumble, and my pussy clenches. I shift my hips to push back into him and give him better access.

I can feel the rhythmic thrusts of his hand jerking his cock. My moans escape me with ease.

"Oh, Jesus, Con, that's hot. Don't stop." I bite my lip.

He pulls away quickly. "Play with your pussy, Will. I'll lick your ass, baby, now you finger-fuck your pussy." Oh, sweet Jesus, this filthy man. I throw my head back in ecstasy as my fingers thrust in and out of my wetness in rhythm with Con's tongue probing my puckered hole.

It's so dirty, so erotic, I'm struggling to remain on my feet. With one hand on the wall, I push my cheek against the wall to help stabilize me.

His whole body is matching the pace of his facial thrusts. He's fucking himself and my ass in sync. I'm enthralled by how erotic the moment is. My orgasm is fast approaching, but I need more. I want more. He's right; I want him!

"Con, I need you. I need you to fill me." I pant in unison with his groans.

"Oh, sweet fucking Jesus, Will." He quickly pulls away as desperate for more than I am. "Fuck yeah, you do! You need me, Will."

He stumbles to get up before slamming his cock into me. "Fuck, that's good. So fucking wet, Will." His cock slams inside me again as he repeatedly draws all the way back and pushes in further. My hips buck in time to meet his.

"Oh god. Right there, Con." My pussy clenches his cock, desperate to hold him inside.

"Too fucking right. You like me tongue-fucking your ass, Will?" The juices drip down my thighs at his filthy words.

His dirty, crazy mouth shoots a thrill through my body, making me unbelievably wetter. "Yes. Oh, fuck. So good." My hand clenches into a fist against the wall.

He pulls me by the hair, his lips meeting mine as he thrusts his tongue into my open mouth. He descends on me like a starved man.

While his thick cock fills me, his fingers dig into my hip, tightening to the point of pain. His balls hit my ass, and the many sensations throw me over the edge.

"Oh, fuck!" he screeches. "Fuck yes, come! Come,

Will. Come on my cock. Fucking own it." My wetness floods his cock.

I throw my head back as Con pistons into of me, ropes and ropes of warm cum coating my inner walls. My throbbing pussy milking his orgasm from him. "Con!" I yell before pleasure overwhelms me, leaving me a trembling mess from the most powerful orgasm of my life.

Con staggers behind me, struggling to hold his own weight with the force from his orgasm, consuming him with ferocity.

"Oh fuck, Will. How the fuck?" He pants and gently kisses my neck. "Fucking incredible."

His soft cock falls from me as he spins me around and cups my face in both hands. "I love you, baby." He kisses my lips with tenderness before pulling away to watch me. His vulnerable blue eyes meet mine, but whatever he sees in mine causes his shoulders to drop and his Adam's apple to bob before he redirects his gaze to the floor.

He steps back and swoops his arm to the floor to tug my panties up and collect my dress. "Come on, Cal only gave us twenty minutes." He smirks.

"What?" I gasp.

Con's playful demeanor is back. "I know, right? No time for round two. Looks like I'll have to wait until we get back to the apartment," he says while pulling my dress over my head.

"Con, I don't think …" He presses his finger to my lips to shush me before removing it and dropping a quick peck to my lips, effectively stopping all conversation, then pulls me back outside as if nothing ever happened.

Chapter Twelve

Con

Dinner with Cal and Lily went well, perfect even. The girls get on like a house on fire. They will give Cal and I a run for our money, that's for sure. Keen absolutely adores Chloe, and watching him interact with her did something to me. It made me want that even more. A baby. With Will and Keen.

Then we can be a proper family, like we should have been.

The determination in me is something I've never felt before. It's fierce. Nothing will stop me. Even Will. She'll come around; I know she will. I just need to show her I'm becoming a better man. The man they both deserve.

"Hey, are you okay?" Will asks, breaking me from my thoughts.

I glance at her, her hazel eyes sparkling and the cute pink blush still on her cheeks from our garage fuck. Jesus, she's hot.

"Yeah. I'm fine." I smile back at her softly.

"You're kinda gripping the steering wheel a little tight." She nods toward my hand. Sure enough, my fingers are white with the grip.

I sigh and brush my hand through my hair. "I've got to meet the guys at the warehouse."

Will's body slumps. "Shit. I'm sorry, Con."

I swallow thickly and try to shrug it off, lifting my shoulder for emphasis. "It's okay. I should be used to it by now."

Will sits forward, her tone gentle and caring. "It's okay, you know. For things not to be okay. You don't have to pretend." She takes my hand off the steering wheel and kisses it, and all the tension in my body eases. How can she have this effect on me? How can she know me so well? She sees me. The real me. And it just cements it in my mind all the more. She's mine. And I'm hers.

———

After settling Will and Keen in the apartment, I make my way over to the warehouse.

Driving the car through the armed gates, I can feel the tension radiating into my neck. My body coiled tight as I shift the car into park.

I glance down at my trembling hands and squeeze my eyes closed, willing the memories away. Anxiety courses through my body. My mouth is dry as I desperately try to gain air into my lungs. My lips tingle, and my heart pounds ferociously.

Shame consumes me for being so weak and vulnerable. I'm losing control. I squeeze my eyes tight and bury my head in my hands, clenching my hair to the point of pain. "Fuck!"

I suck in a deep breath and steel myself before exiting the car and heading toward the warehouse. Each step is like walking to my end, an impending doom, dread.

I feel like I'm outside of my body. Empty and exposed.

A shell of nothingness.

I nod at our security guard and he steps aside, moving his broad body from the doorway.

The thrum of my heart against my chest is so loud I feel like it's echoing through my ears into the empty space. *Thrum. Thrum.*

I can vaguely hear the guys in Bren's office. The laughter in their voices.

I glance at the window. My eyes squeeze shut as my chest vibrates with the rhythm of my heart. Why? My mouth dries, and I struggle to swallow.

Why do I do that?

Why do I always have to look?

And then it hits me, it always hits me, and I suck in a breath …

Six years ago.

Music blares in the car as we head toward the warehouse. Excitement bubbles within me at knowing we can make it in and out before anyone is aware we are there. I glance back at Will in the rearview mirror. Fuck, my girl is hot.

She catches my eye and licks her lips seductively, no doubt remembering why I left my wallet in the warehouse in the first place. I smirk at the memory.

"How the fuck did you leave your wallet there in the first

place?" Keenan asks, completely unaware of the sexual tension radiating off Will and me.

I grin. "I was busy entertaining." I glance at Will. She's stifling a laugh, her teeth tugging on her bottom lip. She's so fucking beautiful.

Keenan huffs beside me. "Seriously? You guys were in there this afternoon? Da would blow his motherfucking stack if he knew!" He exhales sharply, causing me to laugh at his seriousness.

I turn my head away from the road and stare pointedly at Keenan. "He isn't going to know though, is he?" My younger brother and I are tight. We cover for one another, and tonight's just another example of that.

He shakes his head in laughter. "Guess not. So, where to once we get your wallet? I need food!"

"You always need food!" Will leans forward and hits Keenan on the back of the head.

He waves her hand away playfully. "Well, you do too. Since you had that bug last week you've barely eaten; don't think I haven't noticed," he chastises while looking back at her.

Why didn't I notice? Fuck, she's my girlfriend. I should be aware of these things. I drag my hand through my hair in annoyance with myself. I've been that busy with this shit Da has us doing, I didn't even realize my girl was sick. I shake my head in frustration with myself.

I divert my attention. "Keenan's right. Wallet, then food." His grin widens. My little brother is like a mini me, only he has dimples and the ladies call him cute.

Will nods.

I turn the music down as we drive through the gates of the warehouse without issue. Security is always low when Da is out of town and no shipments are due in. It's how I snuck in with Will to fuck her on Da's desk. It was a big fuck you to all the extra *hours he's had me working lately, dragging me into the family business when I don't want to be.*

I park the SUV and roll my head toward Keenan. "Go fetch my wallet, dude."

His face morphs into shock. "Ya kidding me? What am I, your fucking slave?"

"Come on, dude, don't be a cock block." Will hides her face in her hands.

"Fucking Jesus. Give me the goddamn keys. You owe me!" Keenan throws his head back, laughing.

I grin at him, and clasp my hand on his shoulder. "Thanks, bro." I wink.

We climb out of the car simultaneously, but while he takes off for the warehouse, I open Will's door. "What are you doing?" she asks while licking those fucking plump lips of hers.

"Feeding you!" I smirk. "Now get out of the car and on your knees, baby."

I take her smooth hand in mine and help her out of the SUV. As soon as her feet hit the ground, she drops to her knees. Such a fucking good girl for me, she's always submissive and ready. The thought hardens my cock.

Her dark hair is tied into a ponytail, perfect to wrap my hand around. Her hazel eyes shine seductively under the dimly lit car park. I pop the buttons of my jeans and shuffle my Converse forward, my dick straining painfully against my boxers.

I scan around the empty space surrounding us. "I'm gonna be quick, baby, swallow me down like a good girl, yeah?" I stroke her hair gently.

Will nods and opens her mouth. I take my cock in my hands and paint her lips in my pre-cum. "Mine!" I growl. The action alone causes my balls to tingle. I tug her head toward me by her ponytail. She places her hands on my thighs to steady herself. I smirk cockily.

Slowly, I push in through her lips, her tongue flattening to offer me access. Using my hand, I rub my cock along her tongue, in and out, in and out. Fuck, that feels incredible. I close my eyes to the sensation.

"Ah fuck, baby, that's incredible. That's it, suck it in."

I thrust forward so my pelvis hits her as she sucks me down. My hand tightens in her hair, and I use my other hand to steady myself on the car while I fuck her mouth. "So fucking good." I pant around Will's encouraging moans.

A piercing noise interrupts me, making me stumble slightly. My Converse grate on the pebbles around Will's knees, and my senses are on high alert. My eyes dart around the parking lot in panic.

Will's stopped moving and stares back at me with sheer terror, my cock still stuffed in her mouth.

The fear in her eyes penetrates into my soul, and a feeling of sickness washes over me as I quickly pull out of her and begin buttoning up my jeans.

Will jumps to her feet. "Wh-what was that, Con? Was that a gunshot? Was it?" She panics as I straighten myself. I need to calm her down; her chest is heaving up and down, her hands flaying at her sides. "Fuck, Con, you said no one would be here. Shit! She tugs on her head."

My heart races, but I can't let her know, so I take her face between my hands to reassure her. "Hey, it's fine. Probably some of Da's guys shooting their shit out back." I nod at her, and she dips her head in agreement.

Her face pales, and her glazed, panicked eyes meet mine. "Keenan."

One word sends me spiraling into utter turmoil. My fists clench as I gaze back at the warehouse. Shit! I'm so fucking dead for this.

I rush to the driver's side of the car and pull my gun from the glove box.

"Get in the car and lock the doors, Will. Keep your head down."

"What? No way! I'm not leaving you." She stands still, her chin held high. Fuck, my girl is stubborn.

I brush my hand through my hair again; I don't have time for this shit.

I glance back at Will and sigh. "Fuck! Fine, just stay behind me, okay." I grit my teeth, not liking this plan.

She nods, following behind me.

We stalk against the perimeter of the warehouse, following the shadows of the building, and I stop when I hear a commotion at the back of the building.

I pull my phone from my trembling hands, knowing I will be in deep shit for this. I hand it to Will. "Message Cal, tell him to come to the warehouse quickly." She nods eagerly as I walk away from her and make my way through the warehouse door.

It's empty, eerily fucking empty.

I take in the dark room, cold cements floors, and leaky pipes. Nothing out of place.

Yet a sickening feeling is stuck inside my stomach, tugging at me to get out. The hairs on my arm rise, and I sense something is wrong. I scrutinize the surrounding space again with my gun in hand.

A muffled groan leads my eyes to the window. A crate lays overturned as if someone was trying to escape.

Then I see them, his sneakers exposed from behind the crate. Oh shit! My heart plummets.

I rush to him, dropping to my knees. His body is shaking. Is it shock?

"Keenan, what happened?"

He keeps opening his mouth, but nothing is coming out. Panic consumes me. I scan his body. Only now do I see the puddle of blood he's bathed in. Oh, sweet Jesus, no!

My fingers shake as I hold his face in the palms of my hands. A scuffle of feet moving toward me makes me snap my head up to meet with Will's panic-stricken face. Her face is pale and her eyes are wide with fear.

Before I realize what's happening, she's pulled her hoodie off and has it pressed against Keenan's chest. My phone is out, and she's scrambling to get her words out. I don't hear what she's saying. I can only see and hear the trembles of Keenan's body.

Cradling his head between my hands, I stare down at him. He's pale, too pale. His soft-blue eyes are missing their shine. I lean down to his face, noticing something wet on his cheeks. I gently brush it with my thumb, wondering where it came from. Then I realize it came from me, my eyes are leaking. I can't remember the last time they did that.

"The paramedics are on their way. He's going to be okay, Con. Do you hear me?" Her stern, controlled voice has a tremble to it, and I know she's lying, she's only telling me what I want to hear.

I stare into Will's eyes and shake my head, knowing the truth. My little brother will not be okay.

I peer back down at his lips, still trying to move. I kneel further so my ear is next to his lips. "He ... did ... it," he gently pants out.

I pull back to study him, and when I do, a wail erupts from Will. The noise startles me. Her expression is pure devastation. Her eyes trained below me. My body feels like it's floating, like something else is happening that I'm not aware of.

I peer down to see what caused her wail and stare straight into the eyes of my brother. His empty blue eyes. I can't breathe. Air can't get in. It can't get out. I can't breathe. He can't be dead. He can't. I can't breathe.

My hands tremble and my heart sinks. Please God, no. Please help him. Someone help him. "Please." I can't breathe.

"Con. Con. Connor!"

My body jolts, breaking my train of thoughts.

My tight chest hurts. I can't breathe.

"Are you okay?" Oscar watches me with something very close to sympathy in his sharp eyes.

After Keenan was killed, Oscar made it his mission to take over the family security, Da retired, and Bren stepped into his shoes, taking over the office. Cal does the wining and dining with clients, and Finn takes a more hands-on approach. He enjoys the violence, participating in our illegal fight clubs as a hobby. And me? I do whatever they want me to do. Errands, paperwork, overseeing the clubs or casinos. I don't want to belong in this world, but I don't want to let them down either. I can't let another brother down.

"Yeah. Yeah, I'm fine." I nod vigorously, almost trying to convince myself. Oscar's eyes are trained on me as he opens the door to the office. He glances back at me, unconvinced, but I turn away to mask my pain.

I step into the office and fall backward into Oscar when a sharp pain erupts across my jaw.

I wince as my fingers find the sore spot. "What the fuck?"

"That was for Will, you little fucker!" Finn spits at me. His body is bouncing with anger.

Shit. I take it they filled him in on everything, then.

I drag myself farther into the room. Pain radiating from my jaw, I shift it side to side, grateful it's not broken.

The room resembles a boardroom with enough chairs around the table for each of us. Bren sits at the head of the table with his large frame filling the space. Cal, his second in command, sits to his right, looking the part in his business attire. Oscar moves to sit on his left; his white shirt and suit pants make him look the part, with his glasses perched on his nose. He looks every bit the geek he is.

Finn throws himself in the seat beside Cal, and his whole body screams bad boy with ripped jeans and a leather jacket to finish off the appearance. His hair has grown out, shaggy on the top but still shaved at the sides. Not a curl in sight now.

I sit beside Oscar, dropping into the chair with trepidation. I move my jaw from side to side again, testing it. Fucking prick.

I peer straight into Finn's fucking evil eyes. He gloats at me with a smirk. I shake my head and turn my attention to Bren. He nods firmly and begins the meeting.

"Tell us what you have, Oscar," he prompts.

Oscar pushes his glasses up his nose and glances down at his tablet, reading from his notes. "So, it appears Milo has been working with a small Russian gang unconnected to the Dimitriev brothers. Jack and his colleagues are working on a case against them for drug distribution across borders."

I jump in, cutting him off with my angry words. "I want him dead. He hurt Will, hurt Keen, and put a fucking hit on her. Fuck, he tried to shoot us."

Oscar's spine straightens. His voice sharpens, sounding deadly. "If you'll let me finish."

He exhales deeply, then softens his tone. "Now, Da requested he dies. I've worked with Bren and Jack; Jack has agreed that because of the hit outside of Will's house, it wouldn't be safe for Will and Keen if Milo lives. Therefore, he's going to help cover up whatever we do. He's going to pin it on someone else in the investigation."

"Can we trust him?" I shoot out.

Oscar scoffs. "Can you trust the man that took a bullet for you? Am I correct in that, Cal?" His eyes dart to Cal's for reassurance. "Jack took a bullet for Con, didn't he?" Cal nods, and my heart plummets. He's right, he did.

"Yeah, he did. He jumped straight in front of you, Con."

I stare down at the table, fidgeting with my hands in front of me. My tone softens. "Why would he do that? Why did he do that, I mean?" I meet Cal's eyes with vulnerability.

"Because he loves Will and Keen. And he knows how much you mean to her," Oscar explains with no emotion in almost a robotic tone.

How does he know that? The man's a fucking emotional robot. My expression must say what I am thinking, because he rolls his eyes and explains further. "I might be emotionally void, but I'm not stupid. She loves you for some reason, and he knows it will only ever be you. He did it for Will and Keen." I dip my head in understanding.

"So, where the fuck is Milo?" Finn demands.

My eyes shoot up to meet Bren's. He shakes his head. "He's gone deep. Not got a fucking clue where he is. Even his crew are deep. They're avoiding the FBI." He shuffles slightly in his chair. The man is a machine and never shows vulnerability, but now he looks uncomfortable. What the hell is going on? My eyes narrow at him. He drags his eyes up to meet mine. "We're going to need to draw him out."

I erupt. Portraying my best impersonation of Da, and my chair hits the floor with a loud clatter. "Absolutely. Fucking. Not!"

"Calm your shit!" Bren exhales, dragging his hand over the top of his short, cropped hair. "She's not in danger, Con. If you'll just sit down, I'll explain everything."

My heart thunders beneath my T-shirt, and my eyes dart around the table, their gazes fixed on me. I must appear like a wild animal, because that's sure as hell how I feel.

Angered and caged, ready to tear something apart.

Cal holds my gaze and gestures at me to take a seat.

I sigh in defeat, knowing I can't do this alone.

"You're not putting them in danger. I won't have it." I point at them all, needing the last say. They're my family, after all.

"Of course not, Con. Fuck, what do you think we are? We protect our family. Now, come on, screw your head back on. We need you in this." Cal's eyes drill into me, his voice calm and reassuring. I take my seat and sit ramrod straight, glaring daggers at Bren for even daring the words.

"So, may I continue? Is the tantrum over?" Oscar says deadpan.

I spin to face him. My nostrils flaring in fury. He swallows harshly, then clears his throat. "As we were saying before we were rudely interrupted ..." Is he for fucking real?

"There's a charity event on Monday night. It's a Voices Against Abuse event, basically something Will would normally participate in. We are leaving the fact she is going out. But the circle of people who will attend is the same as the last event. The one where she was photographed. So, we know Milo will have people there searching to see if she attends."

"What do you plan on achieving from her going?" I ask as calm as possible, my palms clenching.

"We're basically showing him she's in *our* circle. He knows where to come for her. If he dares come for her. Which he will," Oscar replies with certainty.

"Why are you so sure? I mean, what's it matter to him? Why is he so adamant about hurting Will to begin with?" All valid questions from Finn.

"Will explained that Milo helped dump her at the hospital the night her father attacked her. Maybe he regrets helping her. Or maybe he fears the backlash from us?" Cal muses.

We sit thinking for a moment until Oscar breaks the tension. "Actually, that may well be a reason, but I highly doubt it. That man has a god complex and would quite happily rage a war on us. No, there's actually multiple reasons the man has a vendetta against Will."

I sit taller. What the fuck's he talking about. I scan the room, and we're all listening to him inattentively.

"First, I believe that Will witnessed her mother's death at the hands of domestic abuse by her father. Milo probably helped cover it up." I gasp because fuck, how the hell did this happen? Will said her mother left when she was a young girl. A wave of sickness washes over me. How much was she hiding? How much did she need me, and I wasn't there?

Oscar continues on. "Secondly, Will's grandfather is originally from Russia. Meaning the family have ties

with Russia, hence Will's birth name, Willowmena ..."
Oscar shakes his head at the injustice, his lip curled up
in disgust. "Anyway, it appears Will was due to marry
someone within their Russian ties. An arranged
marriage, of sorts. Once her father found out about his
daughter's"—Oscar shuffles slightly, uncomfortable—
"promiscuity, he couldn't very well pass her off to be
married as a virgin Russian bride now, could he?" He
looks at me accusingly. "He eventually told the Russian
family that Will had been involved in an accident and
died." His voice is void of emotion.

I splutter his words out. "Died? He told them she
died?"

Oscar tilts his head toward me. "Exactly. They paid
good money for Will. They took pity on him for losing
his beloved daughter and settled on a business deal. The
one Milo currently helps with. Now if they were to find
out all this business was built on a lie, then ..." Oscar
leaves his sentence open to our interpretation.

"And finally, he probably blames Will for the death
of his father. According to his headstone, he was broken
without his daughter but now reunited." Outrage floods
my veins. How the fuck dare they treat her like this? My
girl. Mine. My palms clench into fists.

I let out an audible scoff.

Wow, what an absolute clusterfuck. How the hell do
I get my head around this? I run my hand through my
hair.

"So, what? We showcase Will and hope his rats run
back to him with the information?" Finn sneers.

Oscar taps on his tablet, not raising his eyes.
"Exactly that. In the meantime ..." Oscar waves,
gesturing at the door.

The door swings open and in walks Uncle Don. "Evening, boys!" His deep voice cuts through the air, and he slaps me on the back hard enough to make me wince. He's like a fucking bull. "Con, ya little shite, got ya self into a situation, I hear?" he says with a deep chuckle.

I nod and grimace. "Could say that."

"Don't ya worry, me lad. I've got ears to the ground."

My head pops up in hope. "You do?"

He takes a puff of his cigarette, blowing it along the table. "Aye, reached out to a few of my Russian friends. I've given them enough shipments over the years for them to return a favor. They're well aware of how well their loyalties will be paid for information on Milo and his little shites." He flicks his cigarette on the floor, causing Oscar to throw him a venomous glare. Don seems oblivious to the anger and disgust radiating off Oscar.

"So, what else do ya need from me?" he asks while throwing himself into the seat opposite Bren. Now, we have two kings at the table. I roll my eyes at the thought and look into Finn's eyes. He smirks back at me as if knowing what I'm thinking.

He pulls a toothpick from his jacket and chews on it to stifle his grin.

"We're wanting to create a perimeter around Will and Keen until Milo is dealt with. So, if you could take over the security of the warehouse for the time being, then we can use our current men to be undercover and cover the family. Security will be upped for Lily and the kids too. Just until things settle down."

Cal eases in his chair. Shit, I hadn't thought about

how Milo may actually try to get to Will. He could use any of us to get to her. Shit.

"So, you've got yourself a kid, then?" Don laughs.

I meet his eyes. "Yeah."

He nods sharply. "Quite the little empire you lads have got going here. Nice to leave your kids something to run. A legacy." He nods as if he's talking to himself.

"Aye, nice to have a family. Strong lads to hold the fort together." He taps his finger on the table, deep in thought. "Right, I best get going, boys."

We all say our goodbyes to Don as he stands and leaves as abruptly as he entered.

When I hear the final door close, I scan the guys. "He seemed a little deep today?!"

They nod in agreement. "I think he regrets not having a family of his own, that's all," Cal states.

"He's got us!" Bren winks. "Lucky fucker has us!" His grin widens, and his eyebrows dance, making us laugh.

Chapter Thirteen

Will

Con left us alone while he went to the warehouse for a meeting. He told me they had updates from Jack to discuss.

Knowing Jack is okay and working with the guys brings me a sense of relief. I like the fact they're working together for me and Keen.

Con told Keen he had a surprise for him in his gym room, so as soon as we enter the apartment, Keen takes off and an excited squeal comes from the room.

I smile to myself as I make my way to the room next to mine. When I walk in, I gasp at the transformation. Con had clearly hired someone to come in and redecorate the room. It's now a beautifully decorated LEGO-themed bedroom, complete with a *Peppa Pig* toy box. Keen goes wild inspecting the room as I watch him opening and closing the drawers, closet, and toy boxes. His happiness is infectious.

I bathe Keen and settle him in his new bed,

complete with a story and a cheesy smile from my little dude. My heart warms at his little smile and how his eyes struggle to stay open. I brush his curls from his forehead and kiss him goodnight.

Once I'm showered, I await anxiously on the couch for Con to return.

The state he was in earlier made me want to hold him tight and never let go. The vulnerability shining in his eyes took me back to the night that changed him. Changed us.

I can't believe after five years he's still fighting his demons with such intensity. He needs to see someone before they swallow him whole.

The blame and guilt he holds over himself for the death of his brother is agonizing and crushing his soul and heart.

He's pushed me away before, and I know he's capable of that again. It's not something I'm prepared to go through, not with Keen in tow.

Unease spreads through me the longer the night goes on.

Nibbling at my nail, intrusive thoughts swirl my mind. Is he coming home? Has he gone somewhere else? Is he getting high?

The click of the door has me bolting to my feet and rushing over to him. His gaze is on the floor, his body tense. I pull him toward me, and without thinking, I hug him tight. His body relaxes into my touch.

Con's hands band around me, his fingers digging into my spine with the pressure of his hold. His body trembles and his breath tickles my neck as he nuzzles into me. "Thank you." His words soften my encased heart.

I pull back to scan him, and his eyes dart everywhere but at my face. I grasp his cheeks in my palms, forcing him to stare into my eyes. "Are you like that every time you go to the warehouse?"

He swallows thickly and looks away from me while nodding. "Yeah."

I shake my head and hold him tighter, his blue eyes locking with mine. Unsure how he will react to my words, I swallow harshly. "You need to speak to someone, Con. You can't keep going through this. It's consuming you. You're going to snap, and it's going to be at the wrong person."

His guilt-filled eyes dart over my face. Biting his bottom lip, as if holding himself together, he nods gently, and his throat slowly rolls. "I know."

Then he buries his head in the crook of my neck.

"Just hold me, okay?" He sounds exhausted, and his body seems drained.

I tighten my hold on him, then turn my head delicately to place a gentle kiss on his neck. Goose bumps break out on his skin as he shudders into me and the force moves me slightly.

Pulling away, I take his hand. He follows me over to the couches, but I spin on my heel, losing all seriousness as I gift him with a playful smile. I know just what he needs tonight.

He smirks back at me and licks his lips, then I push him to the couch.

He exaggerates his fall and sits with his jean-clad legs wide. His palms twitch beside him as his eyes meet mine, laced with uncertainty. Licking my lips, I drop to my knees between his thighs. I want to give him this, give him the power back, the control he loves, the part of him that lets him be strong. I need to give him this, to help him forget.

I stare into his heavy eyes, and while wearing a cocky smirk, his tongue darts out over his top lip.

"Give it to me, like you wanted to …" I don't say anymore, but I know he knows, by the sharp look and subtle nod he gives me. He knows to give it to me like he wanted to that night Keenan was taken from us.

His voice comes out stern, deep, and ragged. "Take me out."

I shuffle forward slightly, popping his buttons open on his jeans, and he hisses as my hand grazes his hard cock.

He shuffles his jeans down, and I move my hand to the waistband of his boxers, peeling them down. "Will," he warns in a deep rumble.

He lifts again for me to take them down enough to free his throbbing length. His hard, smooth cock hits his stomach and leaves a trail of sticky pre-cum on his chiseled abs. My pussy clenches in response. I move my hands to his thighs before dipping my head to lick his cock and trail my tongue from his balls painstakingly slowly to the tip. He uses his damaged hand to hold it upright toward me, offering me his cock. "Lick the slit. Lick it good."

I stare at him as I lick his slit. He hisses, and I do it again. His eyes burn with desire. He thrusts up slightly, and his other hand goes to the back of my head, his fingers tangling into my hair.

"Again." His voice trembles with grit and need.

I lick it again, but this time, I use my entire mouth to suck the end and swirl my tongue around the head. "Fuck, yes!" His teeth clench as he speaks.

"You're driving me insane, baby. Now suck down my cock like a good girl, and show me what you've got." He smirks. I raise my eyebrows to him and smile around his throbbing tip as I keep my eyes focused on his aroused face, his pupils dilated with need.

I cup his balls with one hand and stroke him with the other as I lick him from top to bottom. Tugging gently on his balls, I swallow more and more of him.

"Fuck, Will."

His hand on my hair tightens as he thrusts up into my mouth. "Gonna fuck your mouth, baby." I nod and hum in response, knowing the vibrations will send him wild. His cock hits the back of my throat, but I take it. "Fuck. Swallow it. Fucking swallow my cock. Fuck. Yeah!" He pants and clenches himself, trying to wane off the impending orgasm, his body rising off the couch with his vigorous thrusts. "Fuck, fuck, I'm gonna …" His hot cum shoots into my throat, and I swallow it all, watching his face ease back into a postsex-relaxed state.

"Come here." He holds his hand out for me, and I take it and rise into his lap as he tucks himself back in onehanded.

I sit on his knee and pull his head against my chest, hugging him. "Thank you," he whispers. I melt against him.

———

I wake to a clatter in the kitchen. Taking in my surroundings, I slowly come to realize I slept on the couch.

Then I remember falling asleep with Con holding me close against his chest all night, my back to his front.

Touching my ear, I remember the tickle of his breath when he told me he loved me when he thought I was sleeping.

"Morning, beautiful. You hungry?" My eyes dart up and catch an amused, bare-chested Con with a kitchen towel thrown over his shoulders. God, he looks hot. My gaze tracks his chiseled body, the wolf tattoo showcased on his left upper arm on full display.

"Are you cooking?" I ask with a quirked brow. Since when does Con cook?

He rubs his hand through his hair, appearing a little embarrassed. "Actually, I kinda bought these." He holds up prepackaged pancakes, waving them in the air. I stifle a giggle at his discomfort. "I got Keen nut-free chocolate, and I saw this site online that shows you how to make meals appear like characters. So, I figured I'd make him muddy puddle pancakes." He shrugs, looking everywhere but at me.

My heart soars at his words. This beautiful man is making *Peppa Pig* pancakes. I tug on my lip with my teeth to cover my smile.

"Sounds great." I smile back at him, his grin spreading proudly across his face.

Chapter Fourteen

Will

We drive the familiar roads to Con's family estate. I'm both nervous and excited at the thoughts of seeing Cyn.

It's been almost five years since I last saw her, and she was the closest person I had to being a mom. The thought of her hurting at me leaving so abruptly or resenting me for not telling them about Keen makes me nauseous. My stomach flutters with butterflies.

As if sensing my inner thoughts, Con takes my hand and gently kisses it. He's slowly working his way back into my heart, and that in itself fills me with uncertainty and anxiety. I can sense him watching me, so I turn my head toward him. "Everything will be fine, Will." Con's blue eyes sparkle with conviction. I dip my head and offer him a small smile before setting my gaze back to the road ahead.

We pull up to Connor's family home. Nothing has changed. The vines are still overgrown onto the roof, and the lawn is perfectly manicured. It feels like home.

A warm sensation travels through my body. This is where I belong.

I get out of the car, and Con unstraps Keen. He strides around to me with Keen's hand in his and offers his other hand to me. He chews on his bottom lip, and when I place my hand in his, his grip tightens ever so slightly before loosening a little.

Heading up to the house, I smile to myself, remembering it's always a hive of activity. As we approach, I can hear the rumbustious noise of Con's family on the other side of the door. Keen hides behind Con's leg, stopping us from walking.

Con bends down and murmurs to him. "It's okay, dude, nothing to be nervous about. Bren's in there and Cal. Little Chloe too. You can show them what a big boy you are today. Can you do that?" I watch the interaction with warmth. Con stands back upright and places his arm around my waist, gifting me with a soft kiss on my neck. "You ready?" he asks with a raised eyebrow.

I roll my eyes to feign confidence, causing him to throw his head back with a laugh and changing the nervous energy between us.

The door swings open before Con's hand even touches the handle, and Cyn comes barreling through, pushing past Con and straight into my arms. I'm squeezed and kissed and looked upon. "My baby. My poor girl!" She kisses my forehead, looking into my eyes. Her eyes are glistening with tears as she holds my arms out to scan me from head to toe.

She shakes her head. "Beautiful, just beautiful!" Then she goes back to squeezing me once again.

"Ma, gonna let up?" Con chuckles behind me.

Cyn's eyes narrow and she spins on her heel as if

she's about to give him hell, but when Keen pokes his small head from around Con's leg, she lets out a mighty sigh. "Oh, my goodness! Look at him." Her eyes snap back at Con with a death glare. She glances away in disgust, then bends down to Keen's level. "Hello there, sweetie, I'm your Nana. Would you like to come inside and have some fresh lemonade? Little Chloe is desperate to see you."

Keen nods shyly.

We follow Cyn into the kitchen diner, the table already full of familiar voices.

A chair scrapes, and pushing past Con is his older brother Finn. He tackles me into a hug, kissing the side of my face. "Good to have you back, darlin'."

I swallow away my emotions. "Good to see you, Finn." He pulls back to scan me. "Your hair's grown." I laugh, covering my emotions.

Finn strokes a hand through his hair. "I know, right? Only took me five years for it to grow this long," he jokes. His legendary leather jacket still smells of weed, and his handsome face has a few extra scrapes, but he hasn't changed a great deal.

"Come and join the party?" He gestures toward the table.

All the greetings from the guys are lovely and welcoming. Brennan greeted me with a hug. Lily explained Reece didn't like to be touched, so I politely introduced myself and Keen, to which he nodded his acknowledgment.

I nodded a small "Hi" toward Oscar because I know like Reece, he doesn't like physical greetings. He smiled at me with his usual smirk and a polite tilt of his head. "Will."

We all sit around the table chatting.

Cal chuckles loudly. "Keen, do you need a cushion or two? You don't quite reach the table." I move forward to peek over at Keen, who is sitting beside Con. Sure enough, his little head barely reaches the table.

Con jumps up in a clear panic. "Oh, shit, sorry, little dude. Let me help you." He rushes off to get some cushions before returning to the table and plumping Keen up on them. Keen is enjoying the attention and laughing to himself.

"You're like a king sitting there, dude." Con grins at him.

Keen grins proudly. "Yep. I'm a king!"

———

We all chat away around the table while Cyn happily delivers the food. She, point blank, refused any help from me. Lily explained she's like this every week. She just loves looking after her family. Chloe sits in her highchair, babbling away, Cal coaxing her to eat with a spoon, then wiping her messy mouth with a small towel. He's adorably devoted to her, and Lily doesn't seem to get a look in.

"I like your fluffy cat, Reece," Keen declares with a mouthful of potatoes.

Reece looks up from opposite Keen, his bright -blue eyes mirror images of Cal's. He's stroking the tortoise-shell fluffy cat that's sitting with its own bowl of food beside his plate, much to Brennan's disgust, who keeps giving the cat filthy looks.

"Name's Pussy," Reece spits out.

Keen tilts his head to the side, his innocent voice

breaking the tension. "Can I stroke your pussy? I love your pussy. It's very hairy."

Brennan drops his fork, Cal and Lily go as still as statues, and Finn chokes on his dinner. I glance at Con, who has tilted his head up to the ceiling, pinching the bridge of his nose. "Sweet fucking Jesus," he mumbles. I bite my lip to stifle the laugh bubbling in me at the change in atmosphere.

I peek at Oscar, whose lip has curled up at the side in amusement.

Clearing my throat, I speak up. "Can Keen pet your cat, Reece?" I ask softly.

He glances up from his meal, oblivious to the change in mood of the room. "Pussy."

I lift my eyebrow in question, unsure what he's getting at.

"You want to stroke my Pussy?" he elaborates.

My words won't come out right. "I … I …"

I gaze toward Con for help, but he's still looking at the ceiling as if that's going to give him answers on how to deal with this. I pass a glance at Finn beside me, his cocky megawatt smile in full force. He's loving this, the little shit.

I sigh in defeat, unsure of what to say next. Luckily, Bren puts me out of my misery. "Reece, let the kid pet the cat." He points the fork from Keen to the cat.

"Reece, don't be so goddamn difficult. You know what you're doing!" Cal chastises in an annoyed tone while wiping Chloe's messy hands.

Reece huffs and mumbles a string of curses, something about us being dicks, it's his cat, go suck cock. Among other lovely liturgies of sentences.

Keen peers at me from beside Con, and I nod in approval.

However, I wasn't expecting him to literally climb the damn table to get to the cat.

"Oh, shit!" Con exclaims as Keen knocks the jug of lemonade over, and the mashed potatoes and peas go flying.

All to stroke the Pussy.

Keen sits on the table as proud as punch, with Pussy on his lap eating the mash from his pants. Con and Cyn rush around, trying to tidy up. Brennan curses up a storm. Bren ignores us all and eats his meal completely unfazed. Oscar taps away on his tablet.

Cal and Lily have surrounded Reece, trying to explain how they perceived him as being difficult, leaving little Chloe happily playing in her highchair with mashed potatoes between her fingers.

I sit back and take it all in, a small smile dawning on my lips.

Finn leans forward in his chair. "Miss us?" he whispers with a chuckle.

Smiling, I turn toward his grinning face. "I hadn't realized how much," I admit, biting my lip. His cocky smile softens.

Chloe continues babbling, but the noise seems to be clearer. I go around to her and wipe her hands with one of the napkins. "What's that, little princess? What are you telling me?"

Her lips pull together, and she blows bubbles, trying to talk. "Pppss."

"Are you trying to say please? Such a good girl," I coo at her sweet attempts.

Lily and Cal stop and watch our interaction. I smile

at them. "She's certainly telling me a story. I'm sure she's trying to say please."

"Pushy! Pushy!" she suddenly shouts, pointing at the cat, her hands clamping open and closed.

I swear to God a pin could've dropped and you'd have heard it. The room goes deathly silent. "Pushy, Pussssy," she repeats clearer. Louder.

Cal breathes in a lung full of air, his face turning to rage, and his chest visibly vibrating through his shirt.

Shit, the guy looks like he's about to have a coronary.

Then he erupts.

He throws the towel off his shoulder at the table. "Her first fucking word! Her first fucking word is pussy?" He spins and glares at Lily, as if it's her fault. His chest heaving, and he's struggling to reign in his temper, that's for sure.

Lily's mouth opens and closes before she shrugs innocently. "It could be worse!"

He glares back at her. "How the fuck could it be any worse?" With his chest rising and his fists clenched, he waits for a response from poor Lily. Her mouth opens and closes again, like a fish.

"I was going to call her Cock." Reece sits back with a smug grin, and Lily spreads her arm out toward Reece as if to say *See*.

"Pussy!" Chloe screeches while trying to shuffle her cute butt closer in her chair.

"That's it! I'm out! I'm fucking done!" Cal all but kicks his chair in and storms from the house. My eyes go to Lily, who rolls hers at his dramatic exit.

"I like Cock!" Keen muses, tilting his head side to

side, looking at Pussy. "It suits her. You're a hairy Cock aren't you?"

Con and I jump in at the same time. "No!"

I shake my head at Keen. "No, sweetie, maybe call her Puss. She likes that best." I nod in encouragement. He pats Puss on the head with a cute smile.

Chapter Fifteen

Will

After dinner, I follow Lily out to the gardens since Reece has taken it upon himself to show Keen how to play basketball on the O'Connell's court.

Cal is on a bench, sitting with his legs and arms crossed on the other side of the garden away from all of us wearing an expression of pissed off and sulky on his face. Yep, definitely looks like he's been chewing a wasp.

"Don't mind him." Lily throws her arm out in Cal's direction while laying the picnic blanket on the ground. I help her out as she places Chloe on the top of it with a selection of toys, which instantly go into her mouth.

I meet Lily's eyes, and she stifles a laugh. "He's being dramatic. Let him have his timeout, and he'll be fine in five."

I peek back at Cal. Yep, definitely looks like he's in timeout.

Lily and I chat away about the kids. She vaguely fills me in on how she and Cal got back together. I cannot believe Reece orchestrated it all. The child is a genius, but by the same token, he's struggled so much in day-to-day life. Lily tells me about trying to get Reece on the right medication, with the right doctor. It sounds awful, and I cannot imagine what it must be like daily for them. Thankfully, they seem in a more stable place at the minute, although Lily pointed out it can all change without warning.

A shadow covers the blanket, and I glance up to Finn peering down at us with a cocky grin plastered on his handsome face.

"What's got you so smug?" I ask him with a raised eyebrow.

Finn's smile stretches across his mouth. "Con just took another fist to the jaw," he says while trying to stifle a laugh.

I gasp in shock. "Another? Seriously? He won't have a jaw left if you lot keep insisting on hitting him there!"

"Would you prefer we hit him in the balls?" He looks at me pointedly, but with the smile on his face, it's clear he's digging for information on our relationship status. I pause, thinking of my comeback but don't get a chance.

"Yeah, didn't think so. Jaw it is." He chuckles.

Finn joins us on the blanket.

He's laid back with his arms under his head, aviator sunglasses covering his eyes, and his dog tags hanging proudly on his chest. His signature black tee has risen, showing off a smattering of hair around his beltline, his impressive golden abs on display.

Wow, I forgot how hot these O'Connell guys are.

Lily makes a noise in the back of her throat, causing my head to shoot in her direction. With her eyebrows raised and a tight smile on her face, I know she saw me checking out Finn.

"So, Will, you ever hear from Angel?" he asks nonchalantly, but with the change in his posture, it's easy to tell it's a calculated move sitting with us.

I smile softly at him. "No, sorry, Finn. I'm still as shocked as you." I sigh in defeat. "Honestly, I expected her back a long while ago." I pick at the blades of grass as I chat to him.

"Did you ever try to find her?" Lily asks Finn directly.

He shrugs off the disappointment, but it's clear in his tone. "Na. If she wanted me, she'd be here. I'm not chasing her. Besides, last I heard, she was happily married." He sits up and stares out at the garden, deep in thought, almost talking to himself.

"Well, I was as surprised as everyone when she went away, Finn. I don't care what bullshit her mom told you. She was crazy about you, and she'd never leave you hanging."

My body breaks out in goose bumps, the entire conversation making me uneasy. Something wasn't right about Angel's disappearance. It was completely out of character for her; she absolutely adored Finn and would never, ever hurt him. No, there's more to it, I'm certain of that.

"Could you speak to her mom again?" Lily suggests.

Finn shakes his head and scoffs. "She died not too long after Angel left."

Bren's loud voice breaks our conversation. "Cal, Finn, get your asses inside. There's shit to discuss." Finn sighs and rises from the blanket, brushing himself off.

Cal stomps across the garden like a petulant

teenager. I can see where Reece gets some of his mannerisms from, that's for sure.

Cyn comes outside a few minutes later, leaving the men inside to talk business as she brings with her some fresh lemonade. I rise from the blanket and join her at the patio table.

She clasps my hand in hers as I take a seat opposite her. Her eyes glisten with protectiveness and love, and I give her a genuine smile and nod in acknowledgment of her feelings.

Cyn swallows down her emotion. "You know, I'm not proud of how my son treated you and his boy …" She glances over at a giggling Keen being chased by Reece. "And I won't try to apologize for the words he spoke to you, Will." I nod at her, so she knows I'm listening. "But when you love someone, you can hurt them with words much more than actions." I incline my head at her and listen to her soft voice. "Those words cut deeper than any knife, hurt harder than any fist, become harder to forgive than any physical reaction. When that person you hurt loves you, you don't forget the hurtful words, but you love them too much to lose them. So instead, you choose to forgive them and move forward. Forgiving them does not mean you forget about the words they said, but you understand that they lashed out with words because they couldn't lash out with actions, and you make the choice to accept it. Those words they spoke probably ate at them as much as they ate away at the person they said them to."

I digest her words. I want to move forward, and I will never forget the words Con said nor his actions, but can I forgive him? I watch my son playing with Reece, his family.

Looking out at the gardens and Lily with Chloe, I know deep in my heart that Con said those words out of grief, anger, and sadness, but I needed him, and he wasn't there.

As if hearing my thoughts, she says, "He's here now, Will. He's here, and tell me, do you really think he's going anywhere else?" Cyn asks as she strokes my hand.

I shake my head at her. No. There's no way in hell Con will ever not be in our lives now.

I peer up at Cyn's expectant eyes and see a fleeting emotion of honesty and experience, as if she has felt the same feelings as me. The same hurt.

"Brennan hurt you?" I ask, my heart clenching for her.

Her eyebrows rise slightly before her body relaxes, and she swallows deeply. "A long time ago, yes," she admits solemnly.

"Do you want to tell me about it?"

Cyn smiles gracefully before shaking her head. "No, sweetheart. Like I said, we don't forget, but we can move on. We can choose to forgive the person, and that's what I did, and I promise you, if you love someone enough to do that, it strengthens your love more than any other action."

Breaking us out of our deep conversation, the kitchen door flies open, and Brennan storms toward his wife. He stands like a mountain above her before bending down and kissing the top of her head.

Cyn peeks at me and smiles gently before Brennan breaks our connection once again. "That little shite will get his balls cut off the next time he steps out of line, sort him the fuck out, Will!" He wags his finger at me in all seriousness, but I have to stifle a giggle between my lips at his lack of realizing he broke up a special moment. Cyn rolls her eyes in jest, making me grin.

I glance up and see Con standing in the doorway, his signature cap on backward, his muscled body showcased in his tight white T-shirt, ripped jeans, and Converse. He's the epitome of hotness.

His eyes find mine, his teasing smile shows me he's aware of me checking him out. I scoff at his smug grin.

Can I forgive him?

I think I already have.

Chapter Sixteen

Con

I've been on edge all fucking day. Scrap that, ever since that fucking meeting at Da's yesterday. It was all going fucking well until we had a meeting while the girls and kids were outside.

I knew we would discuss the charity event that Will and I are attending tonight, but the feeling of not being in control made me act like a bigger ass than usual.

Bren fucking clocked my jaw because I pointed out he's a heartless cunt with no idea what it feels like to lose someone he loves. I mean, Jesus, that guy doesn't want a permanent woman or kid, so how the fuck can he understand how protective I am over mine. Because that's what they are, they're mine! Not the O'Connell family's. Mine!

With other people telling me what's going to happen, and I have no say? Yeah, fuck that.

In the end, I fucking relented. What fucking choice do I have? However, I wasn't relenting without voicing my opinion, even if it meant my jaw would feel like it's fucking broken.

How the hell am I meant to be a great husband and dad with a broken fucking jaw? I mean, it fucking kills to make those damn dog noises Keen goes mad about when I put him to bed. And what happens when I want Will to sit on my face? Fuck, do I want her to sit on my damn face.

Yeah, now I have a fucking hard-on and have to go to this goddamn, motherfucking charity event to showcase Will. Fucking flaunting my girl in front of everyone. I swear to fuck, I'll kill anyone who looks at her. I seriously need a line of coke. Just one to settle me, to make shit easier. My eyes lock onto my drawer, the one I used to keep my party drugs in. I had to empty those when Will and Keen moved in. I could risk nothing hurting them. The realization hits me hard.

I can't do coke.

I don't want to hurt them.

Fuming, I stomp around my room, adding my watch as a finishing touch. I draw my eyes up into the full mirror, and what do I see? Scum. A loser. Hopelessness. I swallow thickly.

A knock against my door breaks my stare. "Con, are you about ready?"

My voice comes out too harsh as I panic out the words. "Yeah, don't come in the fucking room, Will." *Shit.* I tug on my hair. Shit, I sounded like an ass.

She huffs, then I hear her heels click as she walks away. *Fuck. Get it together, Con.*

I take a deep breath and exhale, straighten my shoulders, and turn the knob on the door.

Walking into the living area, my steps falter at the sight of Will standing by the countertop.

Our eyes meet instantaneously. *Fuck, she's stunning.*

Her long legs look even longer when she wears heels, especially with the slit going to her waist. The shimmery silver dress hugs her hips and showcases her tits with its dip at the front. Her long waves are up in a ponytail, and her smokey makeup enhances her hazel eyes. With her lips painted in a plum color, they look a little bruised, and I want to bruise them with my cock. Fuck, how hot would she be with my cum dripping down her chin and coating her bruised lips?

My cock presses against my waistband. *Shit, that hurts.*

"Wow, you look hot!" Will announces while waving over my tuxedo. My lips curl up into a grin when I realize she was checking me out as much as I was checking her out. We're so fucking good together.

The doorbell rings, and I know it's showtime; security is here to escort us. I tense and stand taller. "Come." I hold out my hand for Will. As soon as her soft hand falls into mine, I embrace a sense of calm. My eyes drift to her face one last time before we walk through the door. Her beautiful eyes meet mine, and I lean over and kiss her forehead. "Love you, baby." Then I pull her through the door before her refusal hits me.

I stare out of the window in silence as our driver weaves through the traffic. Will's soft voice breaks through the atmosphere. "Are you okay?"

I clear my throat and meet her eyes. "Yeah, I'm okay. You okay?"

Will laughs and shakes her head. "You've been in a

mood since dinner at your parents' yesterday. What's wrong?" She cocks a brow.

"Nothing." I gaze back out of the window.

She swallows harshly, her voice vulnerable. "Is Milo going to be there?"

I spin to face her and unclip my seatbelt to move toward her, grasping her chin between my fingers. "Fuck no. Jesus, is that what you think? You think I'd let that piece of shit anywhere near you? No fucking way would he be in the same room as you, Will. Trust me, baby." My eyes drill into her, imploring her to trust me.

Her eyes drop before rising to meet mine. "Okay, I trust you. I know something is going on, and you won't tell me, I just didn't know what to think." Her voice is riddled with helplessness.

I release her chin and think about her words. She trusts me. Me.

I study her before giving in. She needs to hear this. "We're going tonight to show you off so word gets back to Milo that you're in town. We have security everywhere, Will, and I won't let you out of my sight."

Her eyebrows rise as she gasps out. "You're using me as bait?"

I tip my head back and pinch the bridge of my nose. "Yeah, I wasn't too happy about it either."

Her soft hand grazes my jaw. "Is that how you got this?" She brushes delicately over the bruising, tingles spreading over me at her gentle touch.

I nod, swallowing thickly at her mere touch. "Yeah."

"You know, I wish they'd stop hitting your face. I kinda like it how it is." She smiles with her top teeth biting into those lips.

"I kinda like those lips of yours around my cock

instead of in between your teeth." I tug her lip from out of her teeth and brush my fingers over her bottom lip. She teases me by licking my fingers before tugging my forefinger into her mouth with said teeth. Then she sucks on my finger, her tongue swirling around. Fuck, that's hot.

My cock twitches in response.

My eyes grow heavy, and I shuffle in my pants, trying to rub some of the ache of my cock against something, anything.

The car comes to a stop and draws us out of the moment. We both pull away from one another.

"We're safe?" Will asks again, her eyes shining with vulnerability.

I bring her hand to mine and kiss her fingers. "Perfectly." She nods.

Security opens the car door, and I step out first before going around the SUV to help Will.

Chapter Seventeen

Will

The ballroom is adorned with white drapes and crystal chandeliers. It looks beautiful. The event tonight is a fundraiser for Voices Against Abuse, a cause close to my heart. I scan the room, looking for anything out of the ordinary.

Con leads us to a round table where Bren and a dark-haired woman sit. Bren rises to kiss me on both cheeks, his stubble catching my skin, making me jump back with a small laugh. He chuckles before introducing me to the woman with bright-red lips sitting beside him in a tight red dress. Bren's deep voice makes me jump into action when the woman, Marianne, holds out her hand for me to shake.

To say I'm a little on edge and not with it is an understatement. I scan the room again. Con grasps my elbow. "Will, chill the fuck out."

"I feel like someone's watching me," I whisper back at him.

His eyes soften on me. "They are. We've got security everywhere. I'm by your side all night, remember?"

I nod and ease down into the chair opposite Marianne, her tight smile watching my every movement as she raises the champagne glass to her red lips. Bren sits stoically still beside her.

The event has numerous speakers and auctions. The O'Connell family have donated a vacation to their luxurious holiday retreat in Barbados. It sold for $250,000. And the proud winner? Marianne. She sits there looking like the cat that got the cream, giving Bren a smug smile and flirtatious lick of her lips before throwing her hair over her shoulder. She makes no attempt to hide her lust for Bren, who does not hide his unfazed attitude. I'm not sure if it's some game they're playing, where he acts like he's not bothered and she does all the chasing? Nope, totally confused.

Con's hand brushes my shoulder. He's spent the entire evening so far with his arm banded around my chair, either playing with my hair or stroking my shoulder. A clear sign of possessiveness. Making it obvious we're together, when really, are we?

"What are you thinking?" Con's voice snaps me out of my daze.

I glance at Bren and then Marianne, who is laughing away and touching Bren's arm while whispering in his ear. The guy is like a stone mountain. He gives absolutely nothing away.

"Are they together?" I ask, a little confused.

Con throws his head back and laughs, drawing attention to us.

He shakes his head, clear amusement on his face. "I doubt Bren will ever be with anyone. I mean, have you met the guy? He's an emotionless prick. I doubt he even cracks a smile when he comes." He waves his hand in Bren's direction, laughing at his own joke while Marianne narrows her eyes at us. I shift a little uncomfortably. It's clear we're discussing them. I glare daggers at Con, causing him to splutter into his wineglass on a chuckle.

Marianne sits straighter in her chair, shifting her shoulders back as if preparing for battle. She swirls her red fingernail around her wineglass. "Sooo, Will, what is it you do for a living?" She raises her eyebrow at me in question. Wow, she's a pompous bitch. She's obviously expecting me not to work for a living.

I smile sweetly at her. "I'm a Family Liaison Officer and Advocate for Domestic Abuse helping families find themselves again. I support them in becoming a stronger unit." Con shuffles forward in his chair before kissing me on my forehead and drawing me into him for a hug. I melt against his chest. "You're fucking incredible, baby," he mumbles against my hair. Something inside me melts against his encouraging words.

I slowly pull away from him. "So, what about you, Marianne? What do you do for a living?"

She sits taller and smiles a megawatt smile before flicking her hair provocatively over her shoulder. "I'm a lawyer."

Of fucking course she is. I almost want to roll my eyes.

I fake a smile. "In what area?" I ask, already knowing the answer.

"Corporate law." She grins. I glance at Bren; he's zoned out. Yeah, there's a reason this woman is sitting beside him, and I'm pretty sure it's nothing to do with her flirting, red lips, and fake tits.

Marianne looks from me to Con, then points her glass in our direction. "So you two are?" She leaves the question in the air with a knowing smile. As if to say, you aren't a couple either.

"Engaged," Con spits out. I almost choke on my saliva. Marianne glances at my finger, my empty ring finger, before smiling smugly once again.

Yeah, I officially want to bitch slap her!

Con has also watched the movement of her eyes; his hand tightens on my shoulder in contempt. He sits forward in his chair, a menacing coldness in his eyes. "She's the only woman I will ever love. Only woman I will ever need. And she will be my wife." He shrugs. "She just needs to come to terms with it."

I don't know whether to be enraged or turned on by his possessive, demanding, determined words. My chest rises and falls with both annoyance and passion.

I flick my eyes over to Bren, who has now taken notice of the conversation. His lip curls up in a smirk at Con's words.

Marianne sees me looking at Bren and quickly puts her hand on his arm, his eyes land straight on it, taking in the possessive action. Wow, this woman is something else. Con has literally sat and poured out his feelings toward me. We've acted as a couple all night, yet she still feels the need to show me Bren is hers? I roll my eyes at her pathetic, desperate move.

Good luck Bren, you will need it.

Bren pushes back in his chair, his deep voice gruff with a tone of annoyance. "I'm going to the bar."

I eagerly jump up to follow him, ready for a break from this table and the conversations surrounding it.

"Me too."

Bren smirks at me, then glares at Con, who moves as if to join me. Bren gives him a subtle head shake that makes him sag into his chair, like he's defeated. Conscious of the bitch over the table, I lean down to Con and press my lips to his. His mouth plunges against mine before I can reach him, his touch desperate, desperate for my lips, for my kiss, for anything I'll give him. The thought makes me clench my thighs from arousal.

Bren clears his throat, snapping me out of the kiss. I jump back, then watch Con's lust-filled eyes follow me as I sashay my way over to the bar with Bren.

Chapter Eighteen

Con

With my girl walking away with my brother, it takes everything in me not to follow, so I grip the arms of the chair to keep myself pinned down, anxiety rippling through me. I scan the crowd, then dart my eyes back to Will and Bren with haste.

"You're coming across a little obsessed, you know? You could tone it down a little." Marianne clucks her tongue in disapproval at my behavior. I scoff. Tone it down? This *is* fucking toned down.

I don't even turn my head to speak to the bitch, I just reply. "That's rich coming from you. If you shake those tits any harder in Bren's direction, you're going to give him a concussion. You're coming across as obsessed yourself. Perhaps tone down the desperation too, not a good look." I challenge. She huffs, and her trap opens, but I zone out because all I see is some motherfucker approaching my girl. Fucking smiling at her. And Will? She fucking hugs him.

Hugs him.

I fly out of my chair before Marianne finishes her sentence. The pounding in my ears intensifies with each step. She's laughing while he speaks to her. Flirts with her.

My temper skyrockets. I stalk across the dance floor, pushing past people trying to talk to me. She's putting something on her phone. His fucking number? She's going to fucking leave me for this prick?

My fists clench and my jaw throbs. My teeth hurt. I see my security team close in slowly as I head toward the bar. His hand is on her motherfucking arm.

I snap the prick out of his gaze when I push against his chest so hard he stumbles back against the stool, sending drinks flying. "Hands off, motherfucker!"

Will gasps beside me. "Con!" She tries to move in front of me, but I don't let her pass. I'm staring the prick down as he glares back at me, waiting to see what move I'm about to make.

Bren jumps in front of me and growls into my ear, "Con, calm the fuck down. This guy knows Will. He's an associate of Jack's. I've been listening in to the conversation, man, nothing to worry about." His eyes drill into mine as if trying to make a point. I relax a little at my brother's words, but my head is still pounding with such intensity it hurts.

The douche sees this as a sign to move away and straightens his jacket. "Willow, hopefully speak to you soon. Have a good night." He tilts his head at Will and turns to stroll away.

"Don't fucking count on it, buddy," I spit loudly in his direction.

As I turn to face Will, I'm greeted with a face of

fucking thunder. *Oh shit.* I scrub my hand through my hair and swallow. "What. The. Actual. Fuck. Was. That?" she grits out while staring at me with venom in her eyes.

I study her, unsure how to handle the situation, moving from foot to foot. Honestly, all I fucking want to do right now if fuck her in front of everyone so they know she belongs to me, but I know she's not down with that.

No, she's expecting some apology or dumb shit, and that's not happening either. I glare back at her and cross my arms in a standoff.

She huffs and stomps her fucking foot before turning on her heel and making her way to the restrooms. I move to follow her, but Bren takes me by the elbow. "You need to calm the fuck down before you cause damage you can't fix," he warns.

Yeah, I don't take advice from someone who's never had a relationship in his life. I shrug out of his hold and go after Will. Bren's heavy sigh leaves me in my wake.

———

Turning into the ladies restroom, I nod at our security detail. Knowing he's cleared the restroom for Will to enter, makes what I'm about to do a lot easier. I smirk as I enter.

Will stands at the sink with her chest heaving, taking deep breaths, no doubt trying to calm down. I grin to myself, how riled up she is. So beautiful when pissed.

When she notices me in the mirror, she darts toward one of the cubicles, and I almost want to laugh at how ridiculous that is. Does she think she can get away from me? Again? My chest bubbles with adrenaline.

I dart into the cubicle with her and slam the door shut behind us, our chests rising and falling with anger, almost in unison. Fucking beautiful.

I cross my arms over my chest in anticipation of her next move. My eyes dart to her purse, her knuckles whitening as she clutches it.

I grab the purse from her and begin rifling through it. "What the hell, Con? What are you doing?"

After snagging what I was searching for, I throw her bag to the floor.

Holding up the offending item, I jerk it from side to side, holding it higher, taunting her. "You put his number in your fucking phone?" I snipe out.

Her bottom lip wobbles as she stares at the phone as if it's a fucking lifeline. She sighs. "He's a colleague of Jack's. He asked me to view some case files for him." I scoff at her dumb reply. That guy wants in her fucking panties, and she's too naïve to see it.

I lean over and drop the phone in the toilet, then flush it.

"What the hell have you done?"

"Pretty fucking sure that was obvious. Flushing the fucking competition!" I point at the toilet.

"I have photos, videos of Keen on there, Con. How could you?" Her voice wavers, but I don't give a shit at this moment in time. I'm too far gone, too hyped up.

I roll my eyes at her dramatics. "Oscar can get them for you," I state. Honestly, I couldn't give a fuck. My brother is a fucking genius. He'll get everything important and anything not? Well, it can fuck right off.

Will's chest moves up and down rapidly, drawing my

attention to her glorious tits, her chest a tinge of red from anger. "You're fucking insane. You've lost it. Absolutely fucking lost it," she fumes, her voice rising.

"Turn around." My voice is calm and a little unnerving even to my own ears.

"What?"

"Turn around." I nod to the toilet door.

Will's eyes bug out when she realizes what I'm insinuating. "Absolutely fucking not!" she seethes.

"Yeah, not the answer I wanted." I lunge forward and grab her hips, forcing her around, then drag her flaying arms above her head. She spins her head around to see what I'm doing while trying to unhook her arms. I grasp my belt buckle with my free hand and unhook my belt, ripping it from my pants.

"Con. Don't you dare!"

My nostrils flare. She doesn't get to tell me no. Not after the torture she's put me through all night. No fucking way.

"Con, I'm not fucking you." Her eyes are ablaze with determination. This just fuels my need for her.

I thread the belt around her wrists and hook her onto the door hook. "Are you wet, Will?"

"No!" she spits out. She's fucking lying. I know my girl, and I know she likes it rough. She likes the games we play.

I shove her dress over her ass. Her motherfucking ass. I could come just from staring at it. My eyes scrutinize it, the toned globes smooth. I palm one cheek, stroking gently before bringing my hand down on it hard. The smack penetrates the room with an echo.

"Shit," she grunts, pushing forward with the force,

but eases back against my hand, and my cock jerks in response to her.

Staring down at her red ass cheek, I realize … "No fucking panties?" The anger inside me bubbles. She's been fucking flirting with some douche, and she wasn't even wearing panties to cover my pussy? *Smack!*

"Ah." A sweet moan from her lips makes my cock jump. I feel the pre-cum wetting my boxers. I ease down my zipper and boxers, freeing my weeping dick and adjust her footing, kicking her legs out and pulling her hips up a little.

"Are you wet?"

"No!" she snipes back. *Liar.*

"Too fucking bad." I spit on my hand and rub it over her pussy just in case, but she's fucking drenched. I laugh tauntingly; I fucking knew it.

Not giving Will a chance to grumble and bitch, I plow my cock in, causing her to shove violently against the door. "Jesus," she rasps.

"Fuck, that's tight." I clench my jaw. Her pussy grips me, molding to my cock. I hold myself still inside her where I'm meant to be.

Nuzzling into her neck, I take in her scent. Fuck, I wish I could stare into those eyes right now. I wish they would mirror my own. I draw back and push again, hard, causing Will to groan.

I grab the skin on the side of her neck with my teeth and pull. She gasps at the pain. "Con. Fuck!" I sink my teeth in farther to mark her. If I could mark her forever, I would.

I continue the process of slowly pulling back, then pound her into the door. "Who do you belong to? Tell me," I demand.

"You. I belong to you."

"Damn fucking right you do." She squeezes my cock with her pussy, making my eyes roll as I fight off the orgasm. Her juices flowing between us, and the sound makes me grip my girl tighter.

"Say you fucking need me," I spit out through clenched teeth. "Say it. Say you'll never leave."

She shakes her head. I draw my cock out of her, and use my right hand to her clit and smack her hard. "Oh, shit, Con."

"Fucking say it, and I'll let you come." Sweat beads on my forehead. My shoulders tense, desperate for her words. Please fucking say it.

She shakes her head, so I take my left hand and draw it up to her throat, adding pressure. I nip at her shoulder. "Say it." Her pussy tries drawing me back in, but I don't allow my cock to move. I want to hammer her through the fucking door, but I don't move. I lick up her neck gently, almost in a caress. As one hand stays on her throat and the other hovers over her clit, I kiss her just below her ear as she melts against me, her head turning into mine. "Please."

I slip out almost on her beg.

She pants out the words I'm desperate to hear, sounding almost broken. "I'll never leave you."

And that's all it takes for me to snap. I push my fingers against her clit and thrust back into her pussy. I'm hammering her against my hand as the other holds her throat in place. My balls tingle, and I can feel my orgasm coming. I growl as I thrust in and out of her, her sweet moans filling the air.

"Cum for me," I demand. Her wetness coats my thighs as my balls hammer against her ass. I stare down at her tight pussy swallowing my cock and pinch her clit, causing her pussy to squeeze me as she screams out my name. "Con!"

My balls tighten at her release, and my cum floods her pussy as I roar her name.

My arms tremble as I work to unhook her from the door. She shuffles her dress down and stumbles forward, but I catch her by the hips. She spins around in my arms and throws her arms over my neck, drawing me down for a kiss.

Her sweet lips meet mine, and I close my eyes and drink her in. This. This is what it's all about. I open my eyes to meet hers, my stomach flipping at the expectation of the usual disappointment in her eyes, but it's not there. My body sags in relief, and before she can change her mind and hate me again, I take her chin between my forefingers. "Marry me!" I rasp.

Her eyes flare in anger. She pushes back from me, and the unexpected shove makes me lose my footing slightly. Her body shakes in anger. "No. Get the fuck out, Con." Her chest heaves as she points at the door, her eyes filled with unshed tears … *What the fuck?*

No? After I gave her an epic fucking orgasm? Seriously?

I need a fucking drink. I'll gladly fucking leave.

I swing the toilet door open; it ricochets off the wall. I storm out the door and nod at the security detail to let them know to stay with Will as I make my way to the bar.

Will

I eventually make my way back to the table while my legs tremble from a mixture of disgust and anger.

I cannot believe Con had the nerve to be so jealous over a fucking phone number. To go as far as flushing the phone down the toilet, fucking me against the door, then being pissed at me because I refused his marriage proposal in a goddamn bathroom, for Christ's sake.

I mean, how the fuck dare I expect better?

What's with the making me face away from him bullshit too? He can't even face me when we have sex now? Am I not good enough?

I feel like shit. Used. Rejected. Utter shit.

I sigh and shake my head at my thoughts as I plonk down in my chair.

Con's chair is still vacant. My eyebrows furrow as I search around the ballroom for Con. Did he leave? My blood slowly boils.

Marianne's smarmy voice cuts through my thoughts. "If you're looking for your future husband, he's over by the bar with his mistress." Her smile fills her gloating face as she trails her finger over her champagne glass.

Bren's and my head snap in the direction of the bar.

My eyes zone in on some pumped-up tramp brushing her hand up and down Con's arm. Her tits pushed into him. He smiles at her and makes no move to stop her blatant flirting. What the fuck? I swallow thickly at their interaction. Hurt grips my throat as I consider my marriage proposal and now this? Yeah, I'm hurt.

"Let's go," Bren snaps before pushing his chair back and gesturing for me to stand. He ignores his date and comes around to guide me out of my chair. My trembling hands grab my purse as Bren pulls me protectively into his side.

"I'll kill the son of a bitch," he mumbles as we weave through the crowd. My heart hammers in my chest as I take one more glance back at Con. His head is thrown back on a laugh. Her hands now on his thigh. Disappointment curdles inside me, sickness rolling my stomach.

No thought as to where I am or what I'm doing.

No thought to the fact his cum is trailing down my leg, making me feel like a whore for fucking him in a bathroom.

No thought at all.

Chapter Nineteen

Con

I fucked up.

Again.

I brush my hand down my face as the light seeps in through the blinds, making me squeeze my eyes shut.

Shit, my head hurts.

The banging from somewhere in the room vibrates around inside my head. Jesus, shut the fuck up already. I wince at the noise.

Slowly, I pry an eye open and vaguely see Will in the kitchen. I grimace at the sound of the blender.

My throat struggles to work as I wilt under her scrutiny. "What the hell happened to you last night?" Her voice cuts through the air—sharp and deadly.

I struggle to sit up straight, my head spinning and my body tremoring. Shit, I'm crashing. What a fucking wreck. I grimace.

I brush my hand through my hair and assess myself. My shirt is open at the top, and my shoes are on the floor. When did I take them off? Where the fuck is my jacket? I scan around the couch, looking for my jacket.

Will plonks a smoothie in front of me. "Figured you'd need that," her no-nonsense voice snaps out.

Will's chest rises and falls rapidly, her cami tight around her breasts, as she gazes down at me with her smooth legs on display in her sleep shorts. Her hazel eyes glisten with hurt. She clears her throat. "You … you, erm, have lipstick on your collar," she all but chokes out.

I flit my eyes away as my hands dart to my collar, trying to remember my night. My nose feels wet, so I brush at the wetness.

Will's gasp causes me to tilt my head up again. The expression of horror on her face causes my stomach to roil. "You're high?"

Shit.

I jump up on unsteady feet and push past her. She follows, hot on my tail. "What the fuck, Con. You're high?"

My legs move toward my bedroom, almost blindly.

"Jesus, Con. I fucking trusted you," she chokes on a sob. "You bastard, I trusted you."

"Leave me the fuck alone, Will!" I slam my door before she can come in and tug on my hair. *Shit.*

Shit. Shit. Shit.

"Con, we need to talk." Her voice is stern and empty of the previous emotion, and the knock on the door penetrates my insides. She needs to talk about leaving me, that's what she's going to say.

My heart throbs painfully, and my fingers tremble. I glance around my bedroom. I fucking hate it. She can't step foot in here. Not here. Not where I've been fucking other people. She deserves better than being in there.

"Don't come in my room, Will!" I all but scream through the door. I don't want her in here. Not here. I go into my bathroom and struggle to turn on the shower with my hands shaking uncontrollably.

I tug off my clothes. Such a fucking failure. I slump against the wall as I come undone. Such a mother-fucking failure.

Will

I've left Con in his pit to fester. His shower turned off hours ago, so I can only assume he's sleeping.

My mind keeps playing over and over the events of last night and this morning. His neck covered in lipstick. I squeeze my eyes shut to try and banish the images. I'm hurting. The man I love, the man I want to build a life with, has betrayed me. Us.

If he's cheated, there's no going back. You don't ask someone you love to marry you, then spend the night with someone else.

Then what about the drugs? Does he have a problem? I can't be with someone like that. I can't have Keen around someone like that. Sickness roils in my stomach. Does he even want us here? He won't even let us step foot in his room. Whenever Keen attempts to go in there, he uses every tactic to distract him.

I shake my head as the thoughts consume me. We need to talk, decide where to go from here, then I can make a plan. With or without Con.

I speak to Lily, who happily agrees to keep Keen.

Bren told Cal about the night's events, who then told Lily. So, they were expecting my call in some capacity or another.

I hear the click of Con's door as I pour myself a drink.

Smooth hands land on my stomach, and I still at his overt movement. Is he kidding me right now?

His breath brushes against my ear. "I'm sorry."

Sorry? Rage fills my veins.

I choke on my words. "Sorry? Sorry for what, Con?" I spin around and face him head-on. His jaw shifts, and his blue eyes struggle to meet mine. "Sorry for fucking me in a jealous rage against a bathroom stall door? Proposing in a bathroom? For storming out and leaving me? Flirting at the bar on the same night you left your cum inside me?" He winces, and his fists tighten beside him. "Sorry for coming home at four a.m.? For not coming home with me?" My voice grows louder. "Or are you sorry for coming home off your fucking face on drugs, Con?" I'm shouting now. "For the lipstick covering your neck?" I choke on the hurt.

"Is that what you're sorry for, Con?" I lick my lips. "Did you sleep with her? Or were you too high to remember?"

He falls back a step, almost stunned, before his eyes meet mine again. Anger glaring back at me with such intensity my heart jumps. "You think I'd fuck someone else? Seriously, Will, you think I'd do that to you? To Keen?"

I shake my head. "I don't know, Con. Truthfully, I don't know what you'd do because everything you've just done …" I shake my head. "It's not anything I'd have thought you'd do. You need help, Con. And if you don't get it soon, it's going to be too late."

"Wh-what's that suppose to mean? You aren't leaving me." His words soften. "Please, Will."

I take a deep breath. "I can't keep doing this. You're all in one minute, then completely detached the next." I lick my lips as I consider my next words before calling him out. "I'm not sure all the things you're saying you really mean."

He scoffs, making a face of mortification. "Like fucking what?"

"You keep saying you want me. But do you really, Con? Or do you just like the thought of having me again. Like the thoughts of a family. We aren't allowed in your room; you don't want us there. I mean, we fuck, but we're just fucking." My voice trembles. "You won't even let me see you. We just screw." I shrug as though it means nothing, but it does, it means everything.

His hand grips my chin, causing me to stare directly into his eyes. They glisten with unshed tears. "You don't think I want you here? Seriously?" His voice raises. "I can't have you in that room, Will." He points angrily at his bedroom. "I don't want you in there—you or Keen." I move to back away, but he pulls me closer. "Will, I can't have you tarnished by the shit I've done in there. I don't want you near any of that." He lowers his head and shakes it back and forth.

His voice wavers as he looks into my eyes, honesty pooling in them. He brushes the hair from my face and tucks it behind my ear. "I can't. I can't see the hurt in your eyes when I have you." My body shudders against his openness. He can't meet my eyes when we have sex because he doesn't think he's worthy?

The question must show on my face because he goes on, licking his lips and steeling himself for another breath. "I can't see the hate, the disappointment, the sadness. Everything I've caused. I can't see it, Will. I want you to want me like I want you." His lips tremble, and his fingers shake against my face.

His words seer into my heart. He doesn't think I want him? Need him? Like him? Love him? My heart suddenly aches for him. To prove to him how worthy I know he can be.

I shake my head; his hands fall away in defeat, but I clasp his wrist and pull him to my bedroom. His body stumbling with me.

The door slams shut as I spin on my heel and stare into his blue eyes. "You didn't sleep with her?"

His face transfixed on mine, there's raw emotion splayed across it. "No. Lena tried to kiss me, and I pushed her off. I called my driver and came home. I was worried I'd had too much and didn't want to regret anything."

"Besides doing coke, you mean?" My eyebrow raises, because if he thinks I'm letting him off with that indiscretion, he can think again.

"Yeah. Besides that." He nods solemnly. His eyes are cast down at the ground, and his voice is low. "I'll see someone about that. It won't be a problem again, I swear." His eyes meet mine before looking away again.

"Look at me, Con!"

He raises his head to stare into my eyes, his dark hair hanging in his eyeline.

I tug my top over my head and throw it to the ground. My chest heaves up and down, and his eyes fill with lust and need.

I glare at him pointedly. "I want you, Con. *All of you.*"

His pupils dilate and he swallows thickly, his Adam's apple bobbing.

I hook my fingers into my sleep shorts and push them down, leaving me naked before him. Con licks his lips. His chest heaving, his palms twitching beside him.

I crawl into bed, placing my head on my pillow and putting my naked body on display for him. He takes short sharp intakes of breath, his eyes glued to my body.

"Come over here and make love to me, Con. Show me how you love me." His eyes flare at my words.

He throws off his T-shirt before pushing down his basketball shorts, and his cock bobs free.

My eyes watch his every movement as he approaches the bed. He tugs his length in his fist, his eyes never leave mine.

He climbs over me, settling between my legs and stroking my lip with his soft thumb. "This what you want, Will? Me?"

With our eyes transfixed on one another; I nod gently. "Yes." I swallow, unsure whether to tell him how I feel, knowing there's no going back once I do. I lick my lips. "I love you, Con. I want you to make love to me."

His body stills, and his eyes widen. I run my hand down his face, then up toward the curls hiding his eyes and brush them away as he stays stoically still.

He chokes, his eyes blurry. "Say it again."

I stifle a giggle and bite my lip. "I love you, you idiot. Now make love to me and fuck me good." I raise my eyebrows in challenge.

His mouth crashes down on mine, and his tongue plunders into my mouth, searching for my own. I meet his kiss; the passion engulfing us both. Grasping his shoulders, my nails dig into his skin as he grinds himself against me bare.

Con's hands move around my body, caressing my hips, breasts, and face. He can't get enough of me. He doesn't know what to touch next, his whole body desperate for me.

"Fuck. I love you so much, Will. So fucking much. I'm going to spend the rest of my life showing you. Proving myself to you. Fucking you."

Grabbing my leg, he lifts it slightly so it's over his hip. He thrusts himself forward, his cock driving into me with such force the bedframe hits the wall.

I peer down to watch him wrap his lips around my breast. His head rises, and he smirks at me before driving into me again.

"Fuck, Con, again."

Thrust.

He grips my breast and twists my nipple, causing me to scream and wetness to pool in my pussy. "Fuck yes, give it to me, Will."

His tongue sets me on fire as he laps greedily at my nipple. He pulls away from my nipple with a suckle, causing a pop. I hiss at the sensation before he dips his head and gently kisses it, followed by a lick. "Jesus, Con."

Con pushes into me hard and deep, and the headboard hits the wall repeatedly. "Tell me again," he demands as he glares into my eyes fiercely, his gaze penetrating through my body. The desire and need in them is almost too much to bear. I clench at the thought, and his moans expose my actions.

"I love you." I tug his head to me by his hair, our kiss

hard and passionate. He grinds into me while moaning into my mouth.

My orgasm builds with each of his thrusts. "You'll never be free. Tell me you'll never be free from me."

"I never want to be," I admit as my pussy spasms around him. My thighs will bruise with the intensity of our love making, but this is me and Con, and we don't do slow and sensual. We do raw and passionate. Desperate and hungry.

"I'm going to …" My orgasm rips through me like a tidal wave. My legs tighten around him to pull him closer.

"Oh, fuck. Fuck," Con chants out. My walls squeeze him and send him over the edge with vigor, and his body crashes against mine with force. Wave after wave of euphoric bliss engulf me as his cock pulses deep inside me.

His forehead falls against mine. "I love you, baby." His eyes meet mine and watch me closely, as if waiting for the change in me.

"I love you too." I smile softly, and Con's whole body relaxes against mine.

He collapses beside me and pulls me into him, his lazy hands stroking down my spine.

Chapter Twenty

Con

Absolute. Mother. Fucking. Bliss. That's what this is.

I lie with Will, her body draped over my chest. My hand trails absently up and down her back. Her hair, damp from our lovemaking, sends chills up my spine. I tighten my hold on her. She's mine, she loves me, and she's never leaving.

I kiss her head, making her sigh into my hold, and take a deep breath. I decide to be honest with her; she needs to know how sorry I am.

I lick my lips, contemplating my thoughts. "Will." She moves so her eyes meet mine, and I swallow the lump in my throat. "I wish I could take back what I asked of you, baby." Her body stiffens, but I ignore it and plow on, needing to get it out. "I was fucked up after Keenan." She nods, her lip trembling. "The shit I said …" My eyes glaze over, and I shake my head back and forth. "I regretted it, but then I heard you'd been to the clinic." I choke on emotion. "I thought I'd done it.

Pushed you to do it. I fucking hated myself, Will. I knew you'd hate me too," I admit.

Will searches my face before laying her head back onto my chest, squeezing me gently, and placing a soft kiss on my heart. "I forgive you, Con." Her words are a whisper, but I hear them, and my arms tighten around her in gratitude.

"I love you," I whisper.

I feel her swallow against my chest. "I love you too."

We lie in silence, both aware that the other is awake. I feel like a weight has been lifted from me. She forgives me and loves me; what more could I every possibly ask for?

"Tell me about your mom," I ask gently. It's something I've been thinking about for a while now but haven't found the right time to talk about it. I guess now might not be such a good time either, because Will's body tenses in my arms. I loosen my grip on her and begin stroking her hip, creating small circles with my fingers.

"She died when I was little. Eight, I think?"

"You don't remember?" My eyebrows knit together.

Will tilts her head up at me, resting her chin on my chest. "I remember her dying. How, why. And after, but no, I don't remember my exact age." She trails her finger up and down my arm, almost copying my movements on her back. "My dad came home from work late one day. My mom commented that his dinner would be cold. He smacked her around. But this time, she taunted him." Will shakes her head at the memory. "She normally never stood up to him. I don't know why she did this time. He turned on her, hit her with a frying pan. She fell to the floor, but he didn't stop there. He climbed on top of her and kept punching her in the face. Over and over." Will's fists tighten as she speaks.

I gently unclench one of her fists and lace our fingers together, then kiss her head. "It's okay baby, I'm here."

She licks her lips and continues. "Milo and I just stood there and watched. We both just stood there, Con. While he was hitting her. So much blood. Her beautiful face was gone. And we just stood there."

"You were a kid, baby."

Will agrees with a nod. "I know. Eventually, I talked to a therapist. I know I was a kid, but I felt guilty for a long time."

I squeeze her hand in understanding.

"My dad got Milo to help him. They wrapped her up in some bed sheets like she was a bag of trash, Con." She sobs into my chest. "She's buried under our porch." My brave girl shakes at the admission.

I tighten my hold on her. He buried her under her fucking house. Under her porch. The sick motherfucker. My teeth dig into my lip in temper.

Will clears her throat. "Milo. He was a teenager. We never truly got along. He's always scared me, I guess. But after that, he was different. Colder. Meaner. I know he suffered trauma too, but … he changed. He was my father's right-hand man, and he loved it." I nod in understanding. The little fucker has been a pain in our asses for a while now, running drugs in and out of our district. Cheap shit. Nasty shit that causes kids to OD.

There was even a rumor going about that he was into human trafficking. After hearing Jack and Oscar's breakdown of the little shit hanging around with the lowlife Russian gangs, nothing would surprise me. And disposing of Will when she needed him? Ordering a hit out on her? Potentially on Keen too? Yeah, the fucker has some sins to repent for. I grit my teeth.

"I'm not going to let anyone hurt you again, Will. I swear it on my life." I hammer the words out with force.

"I know." Her voices softens, and the trust in it makes my eyes close with smug pride. She trusts me, needs me.

"I love you, baby."

She turns to meet my gaze. "I love you too." A smile breaks over my lips as hers descend onto mine.

Chapter Twenty-One

Con

The buzzing noise is annoying the fuck out of me.

"Con, your phone is ringing." Will's sweet voice cuts through my dream.

My amazing fucking dream replicating her on top of me like earlier. Grinding those luscious tits into my chest. "Ah … fuck." I scrub a hand down my face as Will continues to shake me, then grab the phone from her nightstand. "Yeah.

Bren's voice clips through my haze. "About fucking time. We got him."

I sit up straight, the sheet pooling around my cock. "Who?" I question already knowing the answer but needing him to confirm it.

"Milo, you dick. Who else?"

My heart pounds in my chest, my veins pumping the blood furiously around my body. "Where?"

"Basement of Club 11." The line goes dead.

I spring out of bed and begin tugging on my jeans. "Con, everything okay?" I stop in my tracks and stare down at Will. Her hair splayed out on our pillow, her tits on display. The marks on her chest will show every fucker who owns her. Fuck, she's gorgeous.

Do I lie to her? I shake my head. No. We need to be honest. I need to be a better man for her, for them both. I lick my lips and steel my spine, then bend down and brush her cheek with my hand. "They got him, baby. They got Milo."

Her eyes widen, uncertainty seeping through. "Are you ... are you going to finish it?"

I kiss her forehead. "Yeah, baby, I'm going to end this. Then we can start our lives together, okay?" I stare at her pointedly, waiting for her acceptance.

Will nods. "Be careful." I tighten my hold on her head and kiss her lips with bruising force before turning and throwing on my T-shirt.

———

Pounding on the back door of Club 11, I glare into the camera. You'd think the motherfuckers would have had someone waiting here for me. Instead, it's like getting in Fort fucking Knox.

The door opens, and my eyes meet one of our security. "About fucking time," I grunt as I barge past him, making a right turn and descending to the basement.

Bren's bitter chuckle echoes around me as I scramble down the stone staircase.

I take in the room; all my brothers are here. Oscar's sitting at the back with his tablet and raises his cold eyes to meet mine, then dips his head. Cal is sitting in a chair overseeing things. Bren has his shirt pulled up to his elbows. Clearly, he's gotten his hands dirty tonight. He circles Milo, who's tied to a chair in the center of the room. Finn is knelt in front of him, with the knife he holds glistening with blood.

Milo's T-shirt is ripped down the center, a crisscross of cuts marring the skin on his chest, courtesy of Finn's finn-finishing, as we like to call it.

His hands are tied to the arms of the chair. They're disfigured, and judging by the hammer beside Finn, he's shattered the bones in them both. A smile curves onto my face at the thought. Milo's head hangs forward, but his chest still rises. Good fucking job. He's mine.

"What do we know?" I ask no one in particular.

"Informant on the street rang it in. Finn and Bren went to check it out. Turns out he's been hiding out at a crack whore's house." I nod at Cal's words.

I stride toward Milo. Then I grip his hair punishingly, pulling his head back to face me, and his face is a mangled mess. "Did you know about my son?" I spit out. My veins strumming with rage.

Milo chuckles to himself, boiling my blood further. My fists clench on instinct, and the one in his hair almost wrenches it from his scalp, causing him to try and pin his toes to the floor. His defiant eyes meet my own. He spits blood out from between his lips. "I had a hit out on them both." He grins manically, his face lighting up with delight as I recoil at his words.

"Motherfucker!" After I snatch the blade from Finn, I plunge it deep into his thigh before twisting it and taking delight in his screams echoing off the concrete walls.

Milo grinds his teeth. "Did Will tell you how bad our

dad beat her? How he almost killed your kid?" He laughs to himself.

I bring the blade to his face and pull his head back to watch me, his sick grin consuming his face. "She bled like a pig, Con, her cunt bled everywhere," he taunts.

I want to cut out his tongue and feed it to him. I watch him, stunned at his words. "Our daddy tried to sell her cunt. I knew you were fucking her; an O'Connell deflowering my little sister." He laughs. "She tried to deny it. The little whore tried to deny it." I tug his head sharply. "Go on, do it, slit my throat," he mocks, pushing his throat into the knife.

A firm voice breaks my thoughts. "Con." Finn shakes his head at me, so I look at Bren. He nods firmly at me in support. I straighten my spine; this fucker is goading me, but he will not die quick. No, he's going to suffer like Will suffered. Like her mother suffered. Like my son would have suffered.

I lift the blade, dig it in, and slice it down his head, cutting off his ear. It drops to the floor. Milo squirms in the chair, shaking and trying to pull away. His screams should turn my stomach. They should.

I watch in sick fascination as blood oozes down his body. I twist his head to the other side and put my knife toward the other ear, prepared to take him apart bit by fucking bit.

The door to the basement opens, and I glance behind me at the footfalls descending the stairs. My uncle's large frame fills the entryway. "Don." I nod in his direction.

His broad smile fills his face. "Seems ya caught a pig." He laughs at Milo as he squeals uncontrollably. Like the pig he is.

"Let me out of this fucking chair, and I'll have ya, Con. Come on. Be a fucking man."

I laugh at his antics. "You aren't going anywhere, Milo. Apart from hell, that is. After, of course, I've sliced off every limb and taken every organ from your body," I gloat, meaning every word.

He shudders and flails in his chair. "I … I … I've got information. So much information, the Russians. I can tell you everything," he desperately wails. My body relaxes at his heightened state of panic.

The thought of him losing his cock turning him inside out, no doubt. I chuckle at the thought and shake my head. "We don't want or need your information, Milo. And we'd get it anyway, don't you think? You aren't exactly in a position to argue otherwise."

He looks down at himself and probably realizes he is in no position to negotiate.

Then he changes his tactic, laughs, throwing his bloody head back and licking his lips. "You dumb fuckers. Think you know it all, don't you? You don't. You know nothing. Everything you ever thought was a lie."

Bren bristles at his words, and Oscar's eyes shoot up. "Do you know about the connection between the Dimitriev's and Mexicans? You know fuck all!" he shouts jovially.

I draw the blade closer to him, to his hairline, to be precise. I've learned a thing or two from Finn, and how to descalp someone is one of them.

"You betrayed your sister, Milo; you betrayed your nephew, and you betrayed your mother."

I dig in the blade, but the lunatic doesn't stop with his bleating. He laughs through the slice. "You know nothing about betrayal. Look at your own first, Con, the saddest thing about betrayal is it never comes from your enemies. There's a viper in the nest, Con, and you've no idea." His devilish smile taunts. My eyebrows furrow at his nonsense before I peel back the skin from his forehead.

A shadow looms behind me before a loud popping vibrates the walls, causing Milo's body to sag into the chair. My eyes spin around and land on Uncle Don. Bren's body straightens, and Cal jumps from his chair in temper. "Ya as sick as him." Don points the gun in Finn's direction. "There's feckin' blood everywhere. Ya get off on this, ya sick cunts. Shoot 'em in the fuckin' balls and stick a bullet in their heads, easier." He shrugs as if it's nothing. He stuck a bullet between Milo's eyes. Milo's dead. Fucking dead and not by my hands.

I launch at him, but Finn and Bren hold me back. "You bastard. He was mine. Fucking mine!"

Don shrugs off my explosion, tucking his gun back into his jacket. "Got shit to do, boys. Not sitting round here all night while you're creating an unnecessary bloodbath."

"Nobody asked you to come, Don," Cal cuts in, seething. Damn fucking right nobody asked him to come.

Don's accusing eyes hold Cal's hostage. His finger points at himself. "It was my feckin' men that found the bastard. Mine. Not yours, ya ungrateful fuckers."

I sag in Finn's hold. He's right, we owe him. If it wasn't for him and his men, we wouldn't have found him, potentially ever. The thought causes a shudder down my back.

He's dead.

As if hearing my thoughts, Finn clamps me on the shoulder. "He's dead, man. It's over."

I nod. He's gone.

It's over.

Chapter Twenty-Two

Con

It's been two days since we wiped that scumbag off the face of this earth. The euphoria still resonates inside me. When I got home, I held Will as she sobbed with relief, knowing she and Keen are safe and that part of her life is finally closed. She can finally let me in, and we can become the family we always should have been. A sudden wave of nausea washes over me as if questioning if it's really the end? I can't seem to shake Milo's words from my mind. *"You know nothing about betrayal. Look at your own first, Con, the saddest thing about betrayal is it never comes from your enemies."* What the fuck is that suppose to mean? I scrub a hand through my hair. What matters is the here and now. Will and Keen are safe, and they're fucking mine.

Me and my brothers sit around Bren's dining table for our poker night.

It's actually one of my favorite nights, apart from when I'm with Will and Keen. Or deep inside Will, or when Will's sitting on my face, or with my dick in her mouth. Basically, anything with Will or my kid. But yeah, tonight I'm at fuckin' ease with my brothers, and there's only one other place I'd rather be.

"You and Will good now, brother?" Bren asks while dragging a hand over his shaved head. This is as emotional as Bren gets. He's a muscled-headed, emotionless Neanderthal.

I throw some chips into my mouth. "Yeah, we're doing great."

"You start therapy yet?" Oscar's clipped voice asks. He's always the one to put a downer on things. Fucking prick.

I glare at him in response. "Next week, Mom," I say deadpan. He nods sharply as if I've passed some fucking test.

"What exactly is it for?" Cal asks, the concern in his voice clear.

I sigh. Jesus, I just wanted a game of poker, for fuck's sake. I fidget with my cap, spinning it from the backward angle to the front, hiding my eyes, because I fucking struggle to hide the guilt when discussing my brother Keenan. I shrug, trying to act nonchalant. "Will thinks I need to discuss shit about how Keenan died. And she wants to make sure I'm not a fucking addict."

Cal's eyes sear into me. "Are you? An addict I mean?"

I scoff. "No, I'm fucking not. Jesus."

He holds his hands up in defense. "I was only asking."

I sag into my chair and take a pull of my beer. "I use it recreationally, to party and shit." My eyes flare to Finn's because we've used together. He used to help take away his sorrow of losing Angel, and I did to take away the guilt and pain of losing Keenan and Will. Finn holds my eyes, his darkening at my admittance. He knows I won't drop him in the shit, but he still holds me hostage, anyway. I shake my head and turn away, not about to give his secret up.

Cal clears his throat and claps. "Well, I'm proud of you, brother." The table erupts with welcomed slaps on my back, the clanging of beer bottles, and the cheers. Warmth spreads through me, the acknowledgment of their support bringing a smile to my face. My family loves me.

We discuss Keen's birthday. Tomorrow, Will and I are taking him to the zoo together. I can't fucking wait for our first family day out.

Then Sunday on his actual birthday, we are having a birthday party at Ma and Da's, complete with a bouncy castle and shit. I've never looked forward to a party so much. And I've been to some amazing fucking parties.

"So, how's things going with Marianne?" Finn asks, changing the subject from the cards we were dealt.

Bren sighs and strokes his stubble. "Fuck. She's a grade A bunny boiler. Seriously, she wants to permanently jump on my dick." We all chuckle at Bren.

"That woman just wants power. Nothing more," Cal states.

"I'm not so sure. She's wanting a fucking ring on her finger. No doubt about it."

I watch Bren. "You going to give her one?"

His hand goes to his head again, brushing the fuzz. "Fuck no. It's just business."

"Does she know that?" Oscar asks deadpan.

"Pretty sure she got the message last night." Finn grins.

"Fuck, what did you do?" I ask on tenterhooks because when Bren does something, he's like a bull, charging forward with little consideration for those surrounding him, and he makes sure he's heard.

Bren laughs. "I got dinner reservations at the restaurant I knew she had a business meeting at. Took a couple of escorts out for a meal." He shrugs.

I choke on my drink. "Back the fuck up. You did what?"

He rolls his eyes. "She's been bitching about me joining her for this business meal she had going on. So, I thought, fuck it, I'll go, just not with her. Made sure I hired a couple of hot bitches and shoved their tits in her face." I stare from him to Cal, whose eyes are wide open in shock. Finn's laughing his head off, and Oscar is glaring at him like he's a piece of shit.

"Was she pissed?" Finn asks through a stifled chuckle.

Bren shakes his head, laughing. "Man, you've no idea. That'll teach her to not get any big ideas."

"You could just tell her you aren't interested," Oscar spits out, always the advocate of common decency.

"You don't think I did? She wasn't fucking getting it. She wanted to move into my fucking apartment. Even bought herself a fucking engagement ring." His fingers go up to make air quotes. "To make sure she gets the right one."

We sit wide-eyed as he gives us the rundown on Marianne. "I swear to Christ, I told her she's just another pussy. One I also do business with, not to blur the lines."

"How good of you," Oscar chimes.

Bren holds his hands up. "Hey, just explaining I haven't led her on. She comes up with this insane, possessive shit on her own."

"Yes, well, don't go upsetting her too much. We need to keep her a little happy and her daddy very sweet," Oscar says sensibly.

Bren tilts his head and takes a swig of his beer. "Don't worry, I'll stick it in her every now and again to keep her happy. I just don't want her pussy teeth locking me in." We all nod in agreement. A shiver runs down my spine at the thought of Bren being lumbered with that nut job. Hell no.

Finn's voice cuts through the air. "So, which escort agency did you use?" He grins.

Bren throws his head back, laughing. "Indulgence." His eyes shoot to Oscar's, whose narrow on him.

Oscar fidgets in his chair before sitting up straighter, his jaw working from side to side. "And where did you hear about that company, Bren?" he asks with a controlled, sharp annoyance in his tone, as if he owns the damn company I've never even heard of.

Bren raises his eyebrows in challenge. "Actually, Reece recommended them."

Cal splutters. "What! What the hell do you mean, Reece recommended them? Oscar?" He shoots his glare toward Oscar as if asking him to explain.

Oscar breathes out slowly, aggravated at having to explain. "Clearly, your son has been poking around my business yet again," he says deadpan. "Perhaps you could keep a better rein on him? You are his father, after all." He lifts an accusing eyebrow at Cal.

Cal jumps up from his chair. "I'm going to kill him.

Fucking escorts. Escorts! He's barely fifteen. Fucking fifteen."

"He's almost sixteen, dude," Finn chimes in with a smug smirk, correcting Reece's age. Fucking gaslighting the whole situation. That's what he's doing.

"He's a kid. A fucking kid." He brushes his hand through his hair, his chest rising and falling faster by the second. We watch on in amusement as my brother's sheer panic goes into overdrive. He's like a woman on the rag at the best of times. "I need to go … I need to speak to Lily. Jesus, do you think he's having sex with them?" he asks no one in particular as his eyes dart around us all. We all make noncommittal sounds and shrug. I mean, the kid is nearly sixteen.

"Try not to overexert yourself. I'm pretty sure he was poking around and passed the information on to Bren to gain favor of some sort," Oscar states.

Cal studies him, and Oscar's head darts up to look at Cal, an aggravated expression on his face as he explains with a roll of his hand. "I have alerts on my tablet regarding Reece's activities. The boy has vaguely looked at porn, and that's as far as it's gone. I also have a good relationship with the agency discussed, and I'd be made aware of any forthcoming intentions on Reece's behalf." Oscar speaks like he's in a boardroom delivering a presentation.

Cal throws his arms up in the air, spluttering. "P … porn?"

I sit back with my arms crossed, watching the show before me and toss another handful of chips in my mouth for good measure. Bren chuckles into his fist while Finn cracks up laughing at the sheer terror on

Cal's face before asking with a raised eyebrow. "What sort of porn, Oscar?"

Cal erupts. "I'm fucking out. I'm done. Had enough of this bullshit. Don't fucking leave escort fucking shit around my son again, Oscar." He points at Oscar. "I swear to God, I'm done. Fucking escorts! Porn! For fuck's sake." Cal storms to the door, then slams it shut behind him.

Oscar rolls his eyes at his dramatics.

"Seriously, though, what sort of porn?" Finn grins.

"Shut the fuck up, dipshit." Bren hits him around the back of his head, causing him to grunt.

I smile at my brothers.

Fuck, life is good.

Chapter Twenty-Three

Will

We arrive at the zoo for our first day as a family to celebrate Keen's fourth birthday. Keen and Con have matching T-shirts saying, "I'm Roarsome!" on them with a huge tiger face, and they have matching backward caps, jeans, and Chucks. Keen looks cute as hell and a mini replica of Con, who looks hot as hell. I grin inwardly, proud of my little family.

My white sundress floats around me in the breeze. My wedge sandals put me closer to Con's height, making it easier to kiss him as we work our way around the zoo hand in hand.

I'm not sure who is more excited between the two. I take a multitude of photos at Con's insistence. The silly faces and infectious smiles are adorable.

We lean over the alligator enclosure while eating our ice cream, with Keen covered in his. "This has been the best day ever," Keen declares through his melting chocolate ice cream.

I glance at Con and smile. He leans in closer so only I can hear his reply. "Couldn't agree more, watching you lick that ice cream has made my cock rock hard." He grasps my hand and brushes it against his hardness, making me gasp. My eyes dart down to Keen, who is completely unaware of his father's predicament.

I flit my eyes back at Con and raise an eyebrow at his flirtatious smile. Leaning into him, I whisper into his ear, "Later, your cock is going to drip more than the ice cream, believe me, I'll be covered in your cum." I pull back and Con's eyes flare with lust. His eyes dart to my lips, so I give my ice cream a seductive flick of my tongue before covering it with my mouth, mimicking my promise.

Con's mouth parts and a low "Fuck" is muttered. I smile internally at his reaction.

———

The day has been amazing, the weather beautiful, and we're now sitting at the picnic table with our lunches spread out in front of us. I sit opposite Con, and the sexual tension between us is off the charts. We've spent the morning touching one another or brushing each other and passing sexual remarks to one another. Tonight, will be explosive. I can sense it, and I cannot wait. I clench my thighs together in anticipation.

"Which animal has been your favorite so far, Keen?" Con asks while munching on carrot sticks.

Keen removes his cap, sits up a little straighter, and taps his finger against his chin, thinking hard. "Ooo, the monkeys because the tiger was too lazy to do anything."

He makes us both laugh. "He was probably tired and needed a sleep," I explain.

"Nope, he's meant to be roarsome and run sixty miles per hour. He didn't even lift his head to say hi."

Con laughs. "How do you know how fast they run, dude?"

"Reece told me. He also said that daddy tigers can eat the cubs so they can have more babies with mommy tiger."

My eyebrows raise a little s. "Okay, well let's not talk about daddy tigers eating babies."

Con stifles a chuckle.

"When I get a daddy, I'm going to bring him here to this zoo. He's going to love it," Keen states with his little shoulders pulled back.

Con and I stare at one another before Con glances away, his jaw working hard. He sighs out a deep breath and turns his cap around to cover his eyes, and his Adam's apple bobs. Shit.

"And I bet my daddy will love monkeys the best too. And chocolate ice cream," Keen continues, unaware of the change in atmosphere.

My heart races a mile a minute considering what to do. Do I tell Keen Con is his father and risk breaking his heart when he doesn't step up?

Then again, today we have acted like a normal family. Is it really fair of me to keep this hidden? At some point, Keen will find out the truth. I've no doubt about that anymore, and honestly, now is the time for it to be known. Con isn't going anywhere, and if he does, his family sure as hell won't.

I take a deep breath and turn to Keen. "Keen, sweetheart, Mommy has something important to tell you." I glance at Con, but he's facing away from us, staring at nothing, oblivious to what I'm about to say. Keen stops eating his sandwich, giving me his attention. "You have a daddy honey, and he's right here." I point at Con.

Keen's eyebrows furrow, so I go onto explain. "Con was away for a while, but he came back to us as soon as he could. Now that we know he's staying, he's going to be your daddy forever."

Keen's eyes widen, then his face lights up in a smile. "He is?"

"He is, sweetheart."

"Fuck, Will." My eyes meet Con's, his face streaked in tears, his hands shaking. "Come here, little dude." He pulls Keen onto his lap, and they hug one another.

"You aren't going away ever again, right?" Keen asks him.

"Never, dude, I swear it."

I swallow thickly, overcome with emotion as Con buries his head into Keen's thick wavy hair.

———

We drive home in a comfortable silence, with Keen fast asleep after playing tag with Con on the playground, then going into the splash area. We stayed there until the sun went down and Keen was literally dropping.

Con takes my hand and kisses it gently. "Thank you for today, Will. Fuck, I never thought you'd do it, baby." His eyes lock onto mine, then they move back to the road.

"You deserve this, Con, you're a great dad to Keen. You deserve the name to go with it."

Con chokes on emotion. "Fuck, baby. You're killing me here. This has been the best day of my life, you know that?" Vulnerability is shining through in his voice and words.

I pull his hand to my lips and place a kiss on it. "Mine too."

He side-eyes me. "Yeah?"

I nod.

"Better than any outings with Jack?" His insecurities make me want to laugh and scream all in one. I settle on a smile and a nod, and he grins in return.

Con carries Keen to his room, a stuffed monkey tucked under one arm and a tiger under the other.

I head straight for the shower, dropping my clothes to the floor and stepping into the hot water, the heat soothing my skin. I close my eyes as the water cascades over my head.

The possessive touch of Con grasping at my breasts has my eyes darting open, and his naked hardness pushes against my back. His hands fumble with my tits, playing with my nipples. Con pushes his face into my neck and sucks on my skin, causing me to moan desperately.

"Con, you're going to mark me." I panic, thinking of the family party tomorrow and me showing up with a hickey like a teenager.

"Damn fucking right I'm marking you. I'm going to make sure Jack knows who you belong to." My mind slowly registers what he's saying, and the fact Jack will be at the family party is making him insecure. Another reason Keen deserved to know the truth about Con. He needed to realize who his blood family is.

"Fuck, baby, are you wet for me?" He palms my

pussy with one hand while grasping my breast with the other. "So fucking wet for my cock." I moan at his dirty words.

"Turn around so I can fuck you while you watch me, Will." His deep lust-filled voice sends shivers down my spine.

I slowly turn to face him. His pupils blown, overtaking the blue in his eyes, and his cock stands straight, already dripping with arousal. Fuck, he's hot. As if hearing my thoughts, he lunges forward and picks me up. My legs tighten around his waist on instinct as he plunges into me, slamming my back against the tiled wall. He holds me under my ass and leans against the wall with his other arm.

Con kisses up and down my neck and jawline, igniting the passion between us. Wetness gathers inside me as he sucks on my neck. He hits the sweet spot inside me. "Jesus, Con, there. Right there." He swivels his hips, the motion making me moan into his mouth that's now exploring mine.

I grip his ass as he thrusts relentlessly into me. His finger trails down my ass cheeks before dipping farther down. He then pushes it inside my tight hole, making me see stars. I erupt from the inside out. My pussy pulsates on his cock, milking him for every drop of his thick cum. "Ahhhh, fuucckkk Will. Fuck." His body stills, but his cock continues to pulse, releasing every spurt deep inside.

His mouth finds mine again, his tongue exploring mine, and he hardens once again. "Fuck, baby, need to fuck you again." He laughs.

I grab his chin and bring his mouth back to mine; he closes his eyes, embracing me passionately.

Con switches off the shower and carries me through the bathroom into the bedroom. Gripping my hips, he pulls me off him and throws me onto the bed, my wet hair whipping my back at the force.

Con disappears into the bathroom again before returning with a bottle of baby oil and a sexy smirk. I smile at him and raise an eyebrow, licking my lips passionately, and his cock jumps at the motion.

"On your knees, baby."

I smile and roll onto my stomach before pushing up on to my arms, my ass in the air. Con walks behind me. He moans in appreciation. "Fuck, you're incredible." He grips my ass cheek for emphasis, and I push back into his palm, encouraging him.

The cap of the oil flicks open, then the sensation of warmth drizzles down the lower part of my back, seeping into my ass and down to my pussy.

Con's large hands palm my ass, rubbing the oil into my skin. I moan at the sensation.

He grips my hips and pulls me to the edge of the bed, my ass the perfect height for him. His finger trails down my spine before dipping into my puckered hole, and he gently plays with it. Prodding his finger in and out while his other hand caresses my cheek. I gaze back over my shoulder, and Con's eyes are transfixed on my ass. His teeth are nestled tightly against his lip, and the tendons in his neck are throbbing. Jesus, he's so damn gorgeous.

"You let him fuck your ass, Will?" he grunts, his voice darkened.

I shake my head. "I told him I didn't want it."

His finger stops with the prodding. "You saved it for

me, baby? You saved your ass for me like you did our pussy?" His voice sounds of disbelief.

I nod again, not using my words, followed by experiencing the sharp sting of the slap to my ass. "Did you, Will?"

"Yes. I saved it for you," I pant.

"Fuck, yes. You did, baby, you saved your ass for me. I'm going to fuck it so good, baby." he coos heavily with lust.

His filthy words are killing me. "Jesus, Con." I moan shamelessly.

He chuckles. "Yeah, baby. I'm going to fuck you real good."

He adds another finger to my hole, stretching me. "Play with your pussy, Will. Tell me when you're close."

My hand goes down to my clit, and I rub frantically. His hand joins mine, and we rub my wet clit together. "Fuck, that's hot," he groans from behind, his heavy breathing heard throughout the room.

"Con, that's so good. Please."

"Please what, baby?"

"I need more."

"You want my cock in your ass, Will? Say it," he spits out.

My hand twirls around my clit, the wetness gathering. "Oh my god, Con. Please. Please fuck my ass."

"Oh Jesus," he grunts before pushing his cock into my ass with no more preparation or sensitivity. The force of his action pushes me up the bed, but he quickly pulls his hand out from my pussy and grips my hips. The sting in my ass forces my legs to widen to try and encourage my impending orgasm.

"Fuck, baby. I can't move. If I move, I'm gonna

come. So fucking tight." Con talks through gritted teeth. "Keep playing with your pussy, Will. I want you to cum with my cock in your ass."

"Oh shit, Con. Move, please move." My words are desperate.

I stare over my shoulder at him. He's shaking his head. His whole body tight with tension, trying to ease off his orgasm. "Fuck." He breathes through clenched teeth.

My pussy pulsates, and I issue my warning, "Con!"

"Fuck yeah." He moves, driving in and out of my ass. The burning sensation almost overwhelming. I place my face onto the mattress so I can move a hand to my breast and tweak my nipple.

"Fuck, baby, you look incredible with my cock in your tight ass. Fucking come!" he roars.

And just like that, I scream his name as he drives himself home one more time before I feel the pulse of his cock deep inside me. My legs shake at the force of my orgasm.

Con collapses on top of me, his cock going soft inside my ass.

"Fuck. That was incredible." He moves my wet hair to the side of my face, and I can feel him smiling into my neck. "Got all your firsts, didn't I, Will?"

I smile back at his jealous, childlike behavior. "You did."

"Too fucking right, I did. I own you." He rolls me onto my back, making me wince when his dick pulls out of me. His handsome face stares back at me with pure love shining through his eyes. His forehead touches mine as he gently kisses my lips. "Love you so fucking much, baby."

Gently, I kiss him back. "I love you too, Connor." I hold his eyes with the truth of my words seeping between us. His shoulders slacken at my confession.

We smile at one another before he lies down and pulls me into him. With my head resting on his chest, he trails his fingers over my spine as I fall into a deep sleep.

Chapter Twenty-Four

Con

This morning has been truly amazing. I got to witness my son's birthday. The little excitable bundle of joy woke us super early, making it seem like Christmas morning. His excitement and smile are completely infectious. My own cheeks fucking hurt, for Christ's sake, I've smiled that much.

Will and I spent last night decorating the apartment. Animal balloons and banners adorn the room, declaring the birthday boy is four years old.

I made Will and Keen pancakes and even mastered how to create animal faces on them with fruit. Keen's smile lit up his whole cute face.

We watched Keen together as he tore into his gifts. A new scooter, LEGOs, and *Paw Patrol* rescue sets were the main ones. I fucking loved every second of it. I can't wait until later at the party when I tell Will I bought us a house in the same gated community as Cal. It's got a huge fucking garden that's ideal for the scooter. I'm going to install Keen a pirate ship similar to Cal's but bigger, better. Probably a trampoline park or something too. Oh, and he loves water slides, so definitely one of those. Yeah, it's going to be perfect. Best. Fucking. Birthday. Ever.

———

Will explained earlier that Keen and I needed to go and collect a bundle of cupcakes from Sweet Treatz in town while she and the family organized the party, so my little dude and I are now scanning the goodies in the store.

"Daddy …" Fuck, that melts my heart. "Can I please have some of those candies?" Keen points to the self-serve pick-and-mix display. He's bouncing on the balls of his feet. Kid has a sugar rush without the sugar. I smile to myself.

"Let's have a look, dude." I go over to the stand, and as I pick up the paper bag, the bell above the door chimes. Keen breaks out in a huge grin, knowing he's won me over; I smile back at him happily.

"Con, can I speak with you please?" a slurring voice comes from behind me, causing my spine to straighten. Shit.

I spin on my heels and glare directly into the eyes of Lena. Her makeup is smudged, her mascara is oozing down her face, and her pupils are blown the fuck out. Her clothes are disheveled, and she looks like shit. Jesus, I scrub a hand through my hair.

"Daddy." Keen's voice cuts through my analysis of Lena. Fuck.

"Yyyou have a llllittle boy?" she slurs, causing my lip

to turn up in disgust at her even breathing the same air as Keen at the minute.

I turn to Keen and bend down to his level. "Keen, buddy, can you fill your bag with candies while Daddy talks to his friend?" He nods eagerly with a grin.

I turn back to Lena, who is struggling to stand. I grip her forearm and drag her into the corner of the room. "What the fuck are you doing here, Lena?" I drag my hand through my hair. I don't need this right now.

"I need help." Her body is shaking, probably from a comedown.

"No fucking kidding, you look like shit, Lena." I exhale, my words causing her to wince.

"Ple … please Con. Can you get me into a rehab or something? I can't keep doing this. I … I don't know where I woke up today. Can you? Can you please help me? Please." Her voice full of vulnerability and desperation.

Jesus, I can't deal with this right now. I glance back at Keen. He's happily filling his bag with free rein. "I'm scared, Con. I don't think … I'm scared another hit might kill me. My dad, he's thrown me out. You're my only hope. Please." Her eyes shine with unshed tears. The girl is a mess.

Sure, I've never had feelings for her, but I can't just walk away and leave her when I could help. I glance at Keen again, knowing what I'm about to do will not go down well with Will. I stare up at the ceiling and breathe out. Shit, can I really do this? Surely, once I explain, she'd be proud of me, right? I might not have been able to save my brother, but I can save Lena.

My hands tremble with the uncertainty, but when I

look back into Lena's eyes, I know my mind is made up; I need to get her into rehab ASAP.

"Keen, that's enough for now, buddy. Let's pay and get you to your party." Keen turns with a bag full of goodies and nods.

Fuck, this is going to be a disaster. Anxiety ripples through me.

Chapter Twenty-Five

Will

So far, today has been amazing; a crazy, bustling day, but amazing. I cannot wait for Keen and Con to get here. The place looks so incredible. Keen's going to love it.

The gardens at Con's family home have been transformed into a child's paradise. A bouncy castle in the shape of a tiger takes up a quarter of the grounds. A ball pit that Chloe is determined to get into, a face painter, and cotton candy station are situated alongside the tiger castle. Huge bright-colored animal balloons are littered everywhere.

Con's mom has insisted on doing all the catering; she absolutely loves it. The attention to detail on the monkey cookies is incredible. A cake maker has created a masterpiece of a four-tiered jungle cake, and Con has taken Keen to collect the cupcakes as a distraction while we get everything ready.

"My feckin' garden looks like a feckin' zoo!" a broad

voice bellows across the grounds. We all spin our attention toward Brennan, who is standing with his hands on his hips in the kitchen doorway, taking in his surroundings.

"Looks great, hey, Da." Cal pats his father on his back, ignoring Brennan's remarks, causing him to grunt in disapproval.

Cal has been like a hyper child all afternoon, coming up with one elaborate idea after another. Lily has been rolling her eyes at every suggestion. How they managed to have a low-key wedding with his enthusiasm, I'll never know.

I place the multicolored streamers on the cake table as a finishing touch when Oscar declares, "They're here," only vaguely raising his head from his tablet.

I glance over at Jack, who greets me with a warm smile. It disappears when he looks at something over the top of my head. I turn to see where his eyes are fixed, and Brennan is glaring with sheer contempt in Jack's direction. I move over to Jack and brush my hand along his arm in support. His eyes follow the movement, and he faces me with a knowing nod.

Keen leaps from the back seat of the car, causing Cyn to chuckle as we all shout, "Happy birthday!"

We all greet him with hugs, fist bumps, high-fives and kisses before he runs off to join Reece on the bouncy castle.

I wait for Con to approach, but he's holding back, shifting from foot to foot in the same spot by the car. I begin to walk over to him, and the sound of the gravel beneath my feet causes his head to shoot up and his eyes to meet mine. They're completely panicked and vulnerable.

"Con, what's going on?"

Con brushes his hand through his hair in a clear tell-tale sign of nervousness. He glances back at the car and directly at the passenger seat. A slumped body is resting against the window.

My heart pounds. What the hell is going on?

Con swallows thickly, his chest heaving with anxiety. "Shit. I, erm … I didn't want to do this." He waves his hand at the car.

I narrow my eyes. What is he talking about?

As if sensing my confusion, Con explains. "She needs help, Will. I can't just leave her. I need to get her to rehab. She has nobody else."

My mouth goes dry as it registers. The slumped body is that of Lena, the girl who was flirting up a storm with him at the charity event. The girl he did coke with. Lena, the girl he's ditching us for.

He had my son in a car with her? A junkie? His quickie? Oh, Jesus! My legs tremble and my heart races.

"Baby, please don't be mad at me. I'll be gone an hour, tops. I'm dropping her at rehab, then I'm coming straight back, I swear." He steps toward me with his arms open, and I step back.

"You had her in the car with Keen?" I cry out.

His body jolts, as if just realizing that mistake.

"I … I didn't have time to think. I didn't want him to be late for the party. Please, Will, I didn't want to disappoint anyone. Didn't want to disappoint you, Will," he explains, his voice sounding unsure and trembly.

I nod, but my jaw tics in annoyance.

I turn my back as Jack approaches.

"Will. Will, please. I'll be an hour, I swear." I ignore

him and walk toward Jack, and Cal is crossing the garden with Chloe to join us.

The car door slams and the gravel churns as Con speeds away, taking part of my heart with him.

I close my eyes and pull myself together.

"Where the hell is he going?" Cal asks, looking toward the SUV.

"Apparently, he's taking Lena to rehab." I try to mask my voice and hope it sounds indifferent, but I'm sure I fail miserably.

Cal grips my arm to stop me from walking past. "Seriously?" I dip my head, barely able to look into his eyes as I hold back the tears of disappointment. I wanted this to be special. Keen's first birthday with us all, yet his daddy isn't even here.

And as if on cue, Keen comes barreling toward us with cotton candy in hand and a sweaty forehead. "Where's Daddy? I wanna show him how high I can bounce."

"I'm going to fucking kill him," Cal spits, storming away.

"Come on, buddy, you can show me." Jack smiles in my direction as he leads Keen away.

I wrap my arms around myself, sadness and helplessness encompassing me.

A giggle breaks me from my thoughts. I glance over my shoulder and find Jack holding Keen's hands as they bounce happily on the bouncy castle. Yet another sign of Jack's continual support and another stark reminder of Con's abandonment. A shudder runs through my body, the disillusion of us being a family a blow to my heart.

He'll never put us first.

I check my watch again and sigh. We've been hanging on for Keen to blow out his candles on his cake, but Con is still nowhere to be seen almost two hours later.

Looking up, I'm greeted with a dozen sympathetic eyes, all whispering words of disapproval and annoyance at Con. My heart breaks for me, for Keen, and also Con. He's disappointed us all when he promised he'd be someone better.

"When the fuck are we eating cake?" Reece grunts, his eyes transfixed on the cake.

I stare at my watch again. "Can we just give it five more minutes?" I look up at Cal with pleading eyes. His angered eyes soften, and he nods, a struggling smile gracing his lips.

Chapter Twenty-Six

Will

My phone chimes as we sing "Happy Birthday" to Keen. I fumble with it, pulling it out of my pocket with haste.

I don't recognize the number, but I open the message with curiosity.

All the wind is instantly knocked out of me. A photo of Con in the cupcake store with Lena. He's staring down at her with his hand on her arm. I squint at the image; my little boy is in the background helping himself to the treats.

Anger boils inside me. How dare they meet at the sweet store with my son? Is he using drugs again? The girl clearly looks high, a mess. He should be watching our son, protecting our son, not this trash.

"Will, everything okay?" Bren asks, nudging me with concern on his face.

I shake my head and push the phone toward him, unable to speak as my chest heaves in anger. Bren's eyes take in the screen. "Fucking bastard. I warned him to stay away from her. What the hell is he playing at?" he spits, his veins bulging in his forehead.

I walk away to compose myself. The hurt and anger are overflowing, and I need a drink. A strong drink. "Hey, everything all right, Will?" Lily asks as I approach the patio table.

I sit down beside her and a sleeping Chloe. I can't help but soften as I stare at her angelic face sleeping in her mommy's lap. She's normally so attached to Cal.

I shrug. "Disappointed, I guess." She pours me a wine and pushes it in my direction.

"Yeah. I think we all are. We were expecting so much better. I don't understand it. Con's been buzzing all week about this weekend. Where do you think he collected her from?"

"I just got a text with a photo of them together in the cupcake store. I'm so angry with him, Lily. He had Keen with him. If he doesn't want this"—I gesture to me and Keen—"then he needs to say. I can't deal with the childish behavior. It's draining and making me an emotional wreck. I don't want Keen getting hurt either. He's been asking for Con all afternoon."

Lily sighs heavily. "Seriously, if Cal tried any of that shit, he'd have some serious making up to do." She looks at me pointedly.

I laugh almost sarcastically. "Cal is absolutely attached to your kids' hips, Lily. He's more mommy than you." I point out in jest, but if I'm honest, I feel a pang of jealousy at their secure family unit.

Lily throws her head back, laughing. "I know, right? I mean, if he could breastfeed, he would, and boy would I have let him do that, it was hell." She looks out at the garden with an anguished expression on her face, as if even remembering breastfeeding causes her pain. I smile at her.

"Oh my god, no!" she shrieks, jumping up and startling Chloe awake in the process. I follow her line of sight and find Pussy sitting on the tiered cake eating at the third tier with her paw digging in for good measure. Chloe's shrieks jump Cal into action, running over to take her from Lily, her little hands grabbing for her daddy.

"Shoot the feckin' thing!" Brennan shouts across the garden. "Shoot it."

Reece glares at him with hatred. "I'll shoot you in the dick if you touch my fucking cat!" he spits while stomping over to Puss. He gently picks the cat up and nuzzles into its fur. Lifting a chocolate animal from the cake, he offers it to Puss, who licks it daintily, oblivious to the drama.

"Will! Will! *Fuck*, come quick!" Bren's panic ridden voice booms across the garden as I jump up from the chair at the loud desperation in his voice.

Everyone rushes toward Bren, who is on the grass. My heart pounds as I rush to him.

My heart and mind shatter as I approach and find my baby struggling to breathe. "There's something wrong with him, what's wrong with him, Will?" Bren quizzes, his eyes meeting mine laced with panic.

My mind won't work, my body won't process anything, I'm numb, unable to answer as my little boy's chest heaves up and down with a wheeze.

"Nuts," Oscar states. My eyes scan the grass, and sure enough, the candy bag is beside Keen. "Someone call 911. Tell them it's a nut allergy," Oscar dictates as he types on his tablet. Finn walks away with his phone to his ear, his voice loud with fear.

I'm glued to the spot, unable to move.

"Will. Will. Will, snap the fuck out of it!" Jack snaps and grabs my arm. "Where's his EpiPen?"

I can't get my words out or think straight, my eyes transfixed on my baby lips turning blue. He's dying. Oh my god, he's dying. "Will!"

"Table, my bag. Table. Please …" I crumple to the floor as Jack rushes off to the table.

I can hear voices beside me as I hold my baby's hand. They feel clammy. His tiny lips are open and swollen.

"Dad, is he going to be okay?" I can hear Reece. "Dad, make him okay." He's tugging on his hair and screeching loudly.

"Fuck. Lily, for fuck's sake, move Reece." She shuffles away with her arm draped around Reece, consoling him.

Jack kneels beside me, but I'm shaking all over. I can't see clearly through the tears. Jack's frantic hands work on the pen, and he inserts it into Keen's thigh. "Come on, buddy." He gently strokes Keen's face. The wheeze is still audible. "Please, come on," he begs, the tremble in his voice clear, showing his concern.

I numbly stare up and meet Cyn's eyes. She's crying into Brennan's arms, barely able to stand.

I vaguely hear sirens, but my body isn't registering anything other than my baby dying in front of me.

"Someone please help him," I beg. My lips quiver, and my throat is dry.

"Coming through." The paramedics push through us and begin to work on Keen as Jack gives a rundown on what has happened. A frantic barrage of medical terminology and supplies are used as I stand helplessly to the side, begging internally for a miracle. My mind is a complete mess.

Finn stands behind me and pulls me into his side, offering me comfort and support. My teeth tremble in shock, and I whimper through tears. He holds me tighter. "Shh, it's okay, sweetheart. They're doing everything they can. He's going to be fine, I'm sure. He's a little fighter, right?"

"We're going to take him straight through to Emergency Care, you're all welcome to follow behind." One paramedic nods at Bren.

I follow blindly behind the paramedics as they load Keen into the ambulance, Jack guiding and supporting me in beside him.

I glance around the gardens of the party. Only moments ago, it was full of fun and laughter, and now it's a somber sense of foreboding and heartbreak.

The ambulance doors close, locking me in an eternal nightmare.

Chapter Twenty-Seven

Con

Driving Lena to rehab has taken so much longer than I expected. The girl has serious issues, and, quite honestly, it scared the fuck out of me. The drugs have taken over her body and now have full control. Depending on them is too soft a word, they own her. Completely fucking own her.

Lena underwent a full-blown meltdown when I tried handing her over to her doctor. They had to sedate her. I'm drained at the entire experience, and as I get back into my car, I take a deep breath at the thoughts of what I will have to deal with back home.

I only hope Will can see my point of view and is actually proud of me for the decision I made, no matter how shitty the timing was.

I scrub a hand through my hair and pick up my phone.

My breath catches in my throat as I notice the number of missed calls and messages, no doubt calling me out on by a crappy father, husband, and brother. I sigh as I click on the first one.

Oscar: Family emergency call me ASAP.

Finn: Where the fuck are you, dude? We need you.

Oscar: This is serious.

Bren: Gonna fucking kill ya, man. Get your ass home.

Cal: We're headed to St. Thomas Hospital, meet us there.

Oscar: Please call.

Reece: It's Keen. Hurry.

I read the last text, and my blood runs cold. My mind is blank. *"It's Keen. Hurry."* The words play over and over in my mind on a loop.

Jesus. It's Keen.

My hands tremble as I try to call Finn. Straight to fucking voicemail.

I accidentally hit the wrong button as I scroll through my phone to call Cal. No answer. I blow out a breath and a pained noise leaves my body. Desperate.

I try Bren. No answer. I drag my hand through my hair. Why is no one answering? A sickness overwhelms me, the same sickness I felt when my brother Keenan … I swing open the car door, fighting for breath. I can't breathe. I can't fucking breathe. Someone help me. Please, God, someone help me.

My legs shake as I struggle to stand. Fuck, I feel dizzy. Bending my knees and swooping my head down, I take deep breaths. Anything to try and stop myself from vomiting or having a panic attack. My throat is dry, my heart pounding. My legs feel like jelly.

Deep breaths in. Out. In. Out. In. Out.

Slowly, I can feel myself calming. My hands are still

shaking, and I wish like fuck someone was here with me. No, not just someone. I need Will. Will and my boy. Fuck.

The thought startles me into action, and I climb back into the car.

I bite my lip in frustration with myself as I stare down at my phone, trying to make myself take action, to do something, but my mind seems slow on the uptake. Why do I get like this? What the fuck is wrong with me?

Jesus.

I need to get to St. Thomas. I start the engine.

Con

The drive to St. Thomas Hospital has taken me thirty minutes, and I don't even know how I got here. I abandon my car at the entrance. Slamming the door behind me, I race around to the front of the hospital.

"Con, wait!" Oscar's no-nonsense voice cuts through me, stilling me on the spot.

I spin on my heel and come face-to-face with Oscar. A very pale-looking Oscar. He's trembling slightly and struggling to meet my eye. What the fuck is happening? I'm not sure if his behavior is down to his aversion to being at a hospital or whatever the fuck is going on with Keen. I exhale sharply.

"It's bad, Connor, but they're stabilizing him." His voice is full of sympathy.

I jolt at his words.

"Floor six room four."

I nod and rush past him.

The elevator takes too fucking long.

But finally, I can breathe when the doors open, and I push out into the family waiting area.

Everyone is here, all our family. I lick my dry lips and push forward.

The atmosphere in the room stills as one at a time as they lift their heads to meet my eyes.

Bren pushes past the group from the back. I think he's going to tell me what's happened, but then his face contorts into unadulterated rage and disgust. Then his fist hits my face, causing me to fall back onto my ass. I'm overwhelmed with shock; my mouth drops open. Because what the fuck?

"You lowlife, useless piece of shit. Get the fuck out of here before I kill you myself," my brother spits. The veins in his temple and throat are protruding.

My eyes dart away from the tower of a man above me to the whimper of a woman, my mother. Her head is buried in my father's neck, his arms tightly bounded around her. He never holds her in public. Never comforts her. Even when she has one of her "Teddy episodes" as he calls them. The severity of the situation engulfs me. My mind scrambles to piece together what the hell is happening.

My words come out choppy. "Wh … what the fuck is goin' on?" I begin to stand on trembling feet. Finn's hand tightens on Bren's arm, keeping him from me.

Cal steps forward, away from Lily. Her face streaked with tears.

"Where the fuck is my boy?" My heart races frantically inside me. "Where's Will?" I panic as I shake myself down.

"I'll tell you where the fuck your boy is, shall I?" Cal sneers. My brother is normally the sensitive one of the bunch. Our connection normally strong. But not today, not now.

"He's got tubes attached to him. Helping him fucking breathe, Con!" His words come out hurt. His lips quiver. I lick my own lips. "You fucking let him eat nuts. Nuts!" His voice shakes as he turns his back on me to try and control himself.

His words whirl around in my mind. Did I? No. No. I never. I shake the thoughts off. I didn't.

Desperation overtakes me, and shaking my head, I say, "I didn't. I swear I didn't. When the fuck did that happen?" Uncertainty coats every word.

He spins on his heel to face me, laughing condescendingly, then his eyes narrow and his words turn venomous. "When you were with the little junkie slut you rescued today. When you left your fucking son to choose his own candy. He chose fucking nuts!" My heart stops. I swear it stops. My whole body shutting down.

My heart ripped from my chest.

An open cavity.

"He could die." Bren's words cut into me. I can't fucking breathe; my heart has stopped.

"Fucking die, Connor." He points at me. Me, I did this.

My eyes meet Finn's, and he nods solemnly in confirmation. He could die. I choke on thin air. On nothing.

I don't know what to say. What do I say to that?

I hold my body up with my hand against the wall.

"Jack was right, you know. They were better off without you.," Cal sneers the words out while shaking his head in revulsion. His words cutting to the core of my heart. Severing any ties to keep it beating. Any ties of any hope. Hope for my family.

My head drops. A gut-wrenching pain overrides the sickness I previously felt.

Bren's words rage from him. "Get the fuck out of here. You're not wanted here, Con. If Will sees you here, fuck." At the mention of Will, my eyes shoot up to my brothers.

They meet mine with menacing glares. I stare at their bodies. They've created a barrier between me and the room beyond them.

A barrier between me and them.

My boy.

Will.

My family.

Cal's words are soft but firm. Deliberate. "You're not needed, Con. You never were." I suck in a breath.

How am I still breathing and my baby isn't?

Without another thought, I turn and walk away.

Away from my family.

Away from my responsibilities.

My love.

My life.

Chapter Twenty-Eight

Broken, empty, a shell of my former self.

Desperate, despondent, void of emotion.

Con

I walk out the doors of St. Thomas Hospital with a sense of clarity.

The cold air hits me, a chill in the wind reminds me to breathe.

I vaguely recognize a voice calling me from somewhere in the distance. It somehow registers as my brother Oscar's. But I keep walking.

My feet move, one in front of the other. They know where they're going. They don't need me to tell them they're on autopilot.

As I walk through the bustling streets, I feel nothing. Empty, lifeless. Void of feeling. My mind and thoughts don't exist. They're blank. Nonexistent. Nothing.

Bodies move by me. Going about their day-to-day business. The occasional one does a double take. What they see? I'm not sure. I don't care enough to think about it. Maybe someone without a soul. A purpose. Without a family. A life. Nothing.

———

I shut the door of our apartment. The click of the lock engages and reminds me to continue with my actions. The numbness needs to go away. I need to go away.

Cal's words whirl around fuzzily inside my head. *"You're not needed, Con. You never were."*

I gasp at the truth within them. I never was needed.

Bren. *"You're not wanted here, Con. If Will sees you here, fuck."* He's right, I'm not wanted. And Jesus. Will; she'll hate me. I hate myself.

My father. *"She was too good for you, that girl. Too fecking good!"* He's right, she is too good for me. They deserve better. They both do.

Will. *"You leave! You do what you're good at, you turn your back, and you go!"* Will's right, I need to do what I'm good at.

Never needed. Not wanted. Hate. Deserve better. Go. Leave.

My feet stumble to a halt. I struggle to lift my heavy head. Someone stares back at me. This guy. I don't recognize him. His eyes are empty. Black underneath them. His cheek swollen. But it's his eyes. His haunting eyes. I swallow thickly for the guy reflecting back at me. They're empty, nothing left to give.

Nothing left to love.

Useless, worthless, unwanted, filled with self-loathing.

Shattered into a thousand pieces, fractured,
Destroyed beyond repair.
Save me from myself,
I need you to show me you care.

With shaking hands, I open the mirrored bathroom cabinet and sieve through the various products until I find what I'm looking for, the valium I was prescribed when my brother died. When Will left.

When I was alone.

I welcome the darkness.

The emptiness.

I unscrew the cap and close my eyes.

Chapter Twenty-Nine

Will

My hands gently clutch Keen's. His tiny warm hand a reminder of the life within him, and my thankful heart stutters.

The doctors stabilized him. He reacted well to the drugs they gave him and are confident he will make a full recovery. His breathing tubes have been removed, and he's now sleeping. His body resting.

To say it was a close call would be an understatement. I feel overwhelmingly traumatized at today's events, but above all that, I cannot believe my baby is going to recover. My heart quickens when I recall the turmoil of the day.

I push them aside because Keen is here. He's safe, and he will get better. I drop my head into my hands and say another silent prayer to the God I didn't believe in until today.

Movement at the door makes me raise my head.

My eyebrows furrow at the sight before me. Oscar

stands ramrod straight against the door, shoulders tense, terror littered over his face, and sweat dripping from his forehead. My eyes widen at the sight; he's normally so well put together.

I know he has a phobia of hospitals. Something I've always been aware of. But this? This is something else. It's off the chart's phobia. He looks … dreadful.

"Oscar, you didn't have to come. I understand how difficult it is for you."

He holds his hands up to stop me talking, the rudeness of his motion making me jolt.

He brushes the sweat from his forehead, then sneers down at his hand, at his own bodily fluids. "It's not that." He licks his lips before breathing out and explaining. "Well, its partially that. But I wouldn't have come in here if I didn't feel it was abundantly necessary."

I glance down at Keen, unclear with what Oscar is trying to tell me. Keen's over the worst. So why is it necessary to be here now and not before?

Oscar, being the genius he is, reads my mind. "I'm not here for you. Or Keen." *Ouch.* If I didn't know better, I'd have taken offense at Oscar's words. But I know better, and I know what Oscar means is, he's simply here for an entirely different reason.

He fidgets with his hands.

"It's Con, Will." My eyes dart to his, my jaw ticking in anger. He holds up a hand. "Please hear me out."

His jaw moves from side to side. "I've tried talking to them." He tilts his head toward the door, referring to his family. "They don't understand. Con, I mean, they don't understand him, his struggles." His eyes meet mine, and I nod at his words. The fact his family appears completely oblivious to Con's struggles.

Oscar's shoulders relax slightly at my confirmation before he continues on. "He was here earlier. I'm not sure if they told you?" I shake my head. No, they didn't, but then again, I don't want him here. Do I?

I stare down at Keen. He'd want his daddy; the thought sends a pained rush to my heart. His daddy let him down. I rub at the pain.

"Please, Will. I … I'm worried." His words shake, causing my eyes to dart to his.

He swallows thickly. "He left here in a mess. I'm not sure what they said but. Fuck, Will. He didn't hear me call him. He was in a trance. A screwed-up mess. I've never seen him so bad, not even after …" After his brother's death he means but doesn't say it. This is bad. Very bad.

"I've tried to call him." Oscar stares down at his phone as if double-checking it to see if he has any calls.

"I've checked the cameras above his door. He went in, but he hasn't come out." Oscar's face is normally a mask of indifference. Emotionless. But right now, this is the first time I've ever seen despair on Oscar. The thought causes a wave of sickness to flow through me. He's scared for Con.

Well, me too.

I almost choke on my emotion as I utter, "Okay." Oscar visibly relaxes. "Can you come with me?" I ask him, worry coating my words.

He nods dramatically with relief. "Yes. Yes, of course. I'll text Jack. Ask him to stay with Keen." He inclines his head toward Keen's bed. I give him a curt bow of my head.

I cast my eyes down at my little boy and kiss his forehead gently, nuzzling into his curls and scent.

"Mommy will be back soon, buddy. I'm going to fetch Daddy." I smile tightly through my own words.

I only hope I've not just lied to my little boy. I hope I'm not too late.

———

I spend the car journey chewing my skin on the side of my finger. Oscar's hand tight on the steering wheel.

"Do you know what they said to him?" I quiz.

"No. I wasn't there. I don't do hospitals," Oscar states, and I nod. He doesn't do hospitals. But he did for Con.

"Nothing nice would have come from them, I'm sure," he admits. Again, I nod.

"I know you don't want to hear this ..." My eyes dart to his, my jaw ticking in annoyance because he's about to give a speech about how Con's screw up wasn't his fault. Oscar looks forward and doesn't meet my eyes. "Whatever he thought he was doing, he thought he was doing right. I think he was trying to save her." He looks at me pointedly and swallows thickly. "Because he didn't save Keenan."

My breath catches in my throat, and tears fill my eyes. I bite my lip to stifle the sob desperate to escape me. He's right, of course. I shake my head. He was trying to redeem himself.

To be a better man.

I close my eyes and wish the journey to hurry along, my legs bouncing with anxiety.

———

The elevator doors slide open, painfully slow.

I push past them on a mission.

I scan my finger against the security screen.

The door unlocks, and I enter the living room. I scan the room. It's just how we left it this morning. Banners and balloons litter the empty room, Keen's stuffed animal toys sit at the dining table.

Remnants of the animal pancakes Con made for us left on the kitchen counter.

I clutch at the pain in my chest.

"Con?" Oscar pushes past me and heads to the den.

I move swiftly into the master suite. The room Con normally leaves locked.

The door is ajar. I push it farther open and step foot over the threshold.

My heart pounds erratically in my chest as I take in the empty room. It's eerily silent.

"Con?" Nothing. I can hear Oscar shouting his name from the other side of the corridor. No doubt checking my room and Keen's.

I gingerly approach the bathroom, the light seeping from under the door.

I push open the door, and the sight before me causes the wind inside to be knocked from me. I grip my head in agony and shriek. "Oscar, call 911!"

My heart stutters. I crumble to the floor beside Con.

He's slumped on the floor, his head barely propped up against the bathtub. Lifeless.

Tablets are strewn over the tiles. Vomit covers the floor. Con's mouth has a trail of bubbling saliva around it. My hands go to his face. "Con. Con, can you hear me?" My voice waivers as emotion overcomes me. "Pl ... please say you can hear me, baby. Please." I beg hopelessly. My heart crumbles into a thousand pieces, please no. Tears fall down my face, but I ignore them, holding his head up, kissing his hair. Someone please save him.

I'm aware Oscar is beside me, shouting orders into his phone. Then I distantly hear him mention Bren's name, followed by Cal. The urgency behind his voice clear.

I cradle Con's head in the palms of my hands, tracing the stubble of his jaw with my thumbs. There's still a warmth to his cheeks. It fills me with a glimmer of hope. "Please." My tears fall to his handsome face, marking him, a reminder of my love for him. "Please." I beg desperately.

Chapter Thirty

Cal

I sit with my head in my hands waiting for news on Con. When Oscar called to say we needed to make our way from the children's unit over to Emergency Care for Con, to say I was gobsmacked is an understatement. A fucking overdose? He tried to kill himself? I still can't get my head around it.

I mean, I knew Con had been riddled with guilt since Keenan was shot and killed, but this is next level shit. Jesus, how my little brother must have been suffering. We're supposed to protect one another, not do this, not kill him.

I scrub a hand through my hair and scan the waiting room.

Bren is on the floor no doubt feeling just as shitty as me. His knees pulled up and his head hanging low between them. Finn is leaning against the wall staring into space, the fucking toothpick firmly in place.

I lift my head again and eye my brothers. "We should have known."

"Yeah, no fucking kidding," Finn quips.

Bren lifts his head, his tear-filled eyes making contact with mine, and it's the first time I've ever seen vulnerability shine in them. His Adam's apple bobs. "You think he meant it? To kill himself, I mean?"

Finn scoffs and glares at him. "Of course he fucking meant it." He pushes off the wall. "You told him you would kill him yourself." Finn pulls his toothpick from his mouth and spits his words out at Bren, his shaking finger pointing at him accusingly.

"And you, motherfucker." Finn turns on me and strides toward me, and I lift my head and gaze up at my seething brother, his temple pulsating, his face consorted in malice. "You told him we were better off without him!" He shakes his head. "Told him he wasn't fucking needed."

My stomach turns at the harshness of his words, my words. Jesus, I'm a bastard.

I nod and swallow away the emotion rolling inside me, a pit of sickness forming, considering my role in Con's actions. My lip trembles. My words cut him so deep he wanted to kill himself.

The door clicks open, and we all jump to our feet in Will's direction. I scan her up and down, her hair is disheveled, and the poor woman looks broken. Her eyes puffy and red, and her body has a tremble to it. I'd go as far as to say she's in shock. Plain and simple, shock. Jesus. We stand silently waiting for her reaction, but nothing comes out of her mouth, she stares into the room emptily. Is he …? Please no. My legs almost buckle.

As if hearing my thoughts, her head whips round in my direction. "No. Th … they said he's going to be okay."

Relief, utter relief encompasses the room. Our shoulders sag almost simultaneously, and Finn falls into a chair and openly sobs. Bren walks over to him, and in complete contrast to his usual self, he places a supportive hand on his shoulder.

"Os … Oscar's with him at the moment." Will's voice trembles, her eyes seem empty, faraway. Jesus, she's been through so much.

"I'm sorry, Will. Fuck, I'm so sorry." My words spill out of me.

Will's back snaps straight, her eyes punishingly glaring. "What exactly are you sorry for, Cal? Hmm?"

My throat is dry, so fucking dry. "For the shit I said," I admit.

Will nods sarcastically. "For the shit you said? That he wasn't wanted, wasn't needed? Is that right?" Her eyes fill with tears, she wipes them away, but they flow down her face just as fast. Her voice rises. "Well, I fucking want him. I fucking need him!" Her chest heaves. "Keen needs his daddy, Cal. He's only just fucking found him! How dare you say those things to him."

She spins around faces Bren. "And you." She points, then exhales on a choked laugh. "How fucking dare you threaten him, Bren. You've no idea what it takes for him to go to that goddamn warehouse for your fucking meetings every week. To see where Keenan was shot." Her voice rises. "Where he died. We tried to stop the blood pumping out of him, Bren, all the fucking while the life was leaving his body. And you fucking knew how much it hurt Con to keep going there."

Bren straightens, grazing his hand over his crewcut head. "I didn't realize how much he suffered, Will." He turns his face, guilt etched over his stern features.

She licks her lips and continues. "See, I think you did, or maybe you didn't care." She shrugs sarcastically. "You all knew he'd been using drugs, right? As a coping mechanism."

Her eyes scan the room, we all subtly nod.

Finn's wet eyes lift. "He went to shit when you left, Will. We were just fucking happy when he started going out again."

Will wheels back slightly on her heels, and her face turns to rage. Her voice is choked. "When I left?"

Finn's voice is laced in panic as he moves toward her. "Shit, I'm sorry. That's not what I meant."

Her shocked face doesn't budge. "They tried beating my baby out of me, Finn."

Finn tugs his hair. "Fuck, darlin'. I know, I'm sorry. I'm not blaming you. I swear." He puts his hands out and steps toward her. She holds her hands up to stop him, and I move in, ready to go between them, when my eyes latch onto Bren's, and he subtly shakes his head.

"I went through all that shit. Dealt with all that shit. Was thrown to the fucking wolves by Con. The man I loved and adored since we were kids." Her finger points at her chest, emotion and anger rolling off her in waves, and her voice quivering but somehow still strong. "And yet here I stand, supporting him like you should have." She points back at Finn. "And you." She points at Bren, then turns her head toward me. "And you, Cal. He supported you, he rooted for you! You should have done the same for him."

Her legs buckle, and I swoop in and catch her, and she rests her head against my chest and sobs rack through her body. She feels fragile in my arms. This sweet girl has been through hell and back, yet still always had our brother's back. She's been his lifeline until we took that away from him. Destroyed him.

I sit with her limp body, cradling her in my arms. "You're right, sweetheart. We let him down and destroyed him. We're going to prove to you both we're here for you. Both of you." I stroke her hair.

Will raises her head, her face mottled with sadness and desperation seeping through her words. "He needs help, Cal."

"We're going to fucking get it for him, Will. Promise ya." Bren's firm voice is low a contrast to his normal deep and demanding tone.

"Ain't ever gonna let this shit happen again, Will, promise ya that." Finn's concerned eyes meet mine, and I nod. Never.

We'll never hurt him like that again. And we'll kill any fucker who dares to try.

Chapter Thirty-One

Build me, help me, love my broken self,

Hold me through this misery.

Take away the pain,

Support me to stand, to feel once again.

Con

The irritating beeping and buzzing hurts my head. What the fuck? I lick my lips; they're dry and cracked. I try to swallow, but the roughness and sharp sting in my throat make it difficult. What the fuck happened?

My eyes are closed, and I will them to open, but they don't. Are they locked? I feel locked in. Where the hell am I?

My mind tries to recall what might be happening.

How I came to be like this. Small flashes of Keen munching on his pancakes flash before me. Balloons, gifts. His birthday. I smile internally at his cute face while opening his presents. My own feelings of excitement and joy flood my veins. Then, like an impending doom, sadness and darkness hit me. Keen. Nuts. Hospital. Failure. Losing them. Both of them. My family.

I wail, a gut-wrenching, ear-shrieking wail.

My eyes shoot open to the whiteness of the room. I'm alive. Fuck no. I'm alive.

"Shh. Shh. It's okay ,baby, I've got you," a gentle voice coos, calming me, my body gently floats back down to the bed as Will's hands soothe me all over. Her fingers stroke my face, over my stubble, up to my eyes. "Open your eyes, Con, I need to see you, baby, please." The vulnerability and desperation in her voice leaves me no alternative. I'd give this woman anything. Any-fucking-thing she wants.

Her beautiful hazel eyes glisten with tears. She maneuvers herself onto the bed beside me. I shuffle back slightly, and she climbs in. Her head is resting on the same pillow as mine. We watch each other. Her hands entwine with mine. Hers encapsulating mine into a fierce grip, where mine can barely hold hers. A complete contrast to our usual stance. Her strength holding my weakness. Again, another reminder.

I close my eyes. I'm not good enough. I need to be strong for her.

"Open your eyes, Con," she coaxes.

I open them straight away, almost submissively. She licks her lips, ducking her head and swallowing hard. I watch the motion. "You scared me." My jaw tenses and I wince. She gently touches my jaw. "I love you. So much …" Her words come out smothered by emotion, and tears race down her face. "Promise me you'll never do that again." Her eyes glare into me pointedly, her tone serious and sharp. "Promise me!"

I lick my lips but don't give her the answer she wants. Because without her, without Keen? I'd rather die. I'm nothing without them. Nothing.

"Keen?"

"He's fine."

I choke on a breath, my heart skipping. I want to keel over and bawl in relief.

The wetness flows freely down my face.

"He's okay, Con. You're okay. We're going to be okay." Her hand brushes away my tears.

My voice trembles. "I thought …"

Will squeezes her eyes closed in pain. "Shh, shh. I know what you thought." Her hands stroke up and down my arm. "I know, it's okay. We're going to be okay."

"I … I … can't do this without you, Will." My voice is coming out desperate, pleading, pathetic.

Her gentle voice caresses me, like a mother would to a child. "I know. I can't do this without you either." The impact of her words consumes me. Does she still want me? I dart my eyes up to meet hers in question.

Will leans forward and lightly kisses my lips. "I love you. We're going to get you help, Con. You're going to get better, stronger. Then I'm going to marry you. We're going to live in that big house Cal told me about and have a puppy running around the big garden. And Keen's going to get the biggest play structure on the block." Her voice is teasing as she tries to smile through her pain, through her tears.

My slow mind goes over her words. She still wants me. Loves me. We're going to be a family. Stronger.

Her arms band around me, and I tighten my hold on her.

"I love you, baby. So fucking much it hurts," I admit.

"I know. I love you too."

Rebuild me, fill me with love and kindness,
Show me that you're there.
Safe in your loving arms, comfort all around me.
Save me for myself.

———

We hold each other and just stare into one another's eyes. The connection between us doesn't need words. Our connection is everything we need. Love.

I'm not sure how long we lie like this, feels like hours. Days even. Not long enough. It'll never be long enough.

I wet my lips with my tongue. "You really want a puppy with me?" I ask her with a coy smile.

Her pretty, hazel eyes light up in amusement. "I do."

"Fuck, baby. This is big. I'm going to be a daddy again."

Will chokes on a laugh and bites her lip, the action making her even more beautiful. "A doggy daddy, yes."

I shrug slightly. "Yeah. Same thing. Still a daddy."

"It is." She giggles. The noise warms me inside out. She brushes the wayward hair from my face. Her fingertips leave behind the softness she exudes. Her gentle caress and warmth.

Her love.

Chapter Thirty-Two

Will

Con's brothers have been distant all day. The realization pisses me off, causing my head to pound with the tension. I can feel Con's wavering uncertainty around the situation, but I'm standing tall and beside my man. He's got my full support, and I won't let anyone knock him down. I feel like a mother protecting her cub.

My arms are crossed over my chest as I sit guard at Con's bedside. He's been in and out of sleep all day after we spent the night holding one another.

As if hearing my thoughts, the door gently opens, and my eyes shoot over to it. Bren, Finn, and Cal slowly approach the bed.

"Jesus." Cal chokes and falls to the chair beside Con. His hands shake as he moves them toward him. They stop, and his eyes meet mine in question. I nod, and he relaxes slightly, gently taking Con's hand in his. The motion makes my heart ache.

"Will." Bren's voice is soft and insecure. My eyes

meet his. Tears blur my vision as I take in Bren's pained face. "I'm sorry, darlin'. I didn't realize he felt this way." His voice rises. "Fuck! The things I said." He scrubs a hand through his buzz cut head.

"I deserved them," Con muffles the words out, his eyes fluttering open.

Bren shakes his head violently, silently raging at himself. At his actions. "No, man. We should have been there. Seen you struggle. Jesus, who am I kidding? We knew you'd struggled since Keenan. And Will." He clears his throat. "We're here now, man. We're here for whatever you need." He nods.

"Gonna, need some time off." Con moves to sit up slightly. Cal's hand still in his. His brothers watch him and wait for him to elaborate. "Gonna be a daddy." My eyes bug out.

Cal chokes and winces. Bren looks borderline aggressive, struggling to rein in his true feelings, and Finn stands at the door with a toothpick in his mouth with a megawatt, troublemaking grin.

I decide to clarify as I watch them all uncomfortably, trying not to give too much emotion away. I take pity on them. "He means we're going to have a puppy." I point at Con in jest. "When we're fully moved in the house." His face is alight, and he grins from ear to ear. His eyes dart around his brother before he cracks up laughing.

They all visibly exhale, followed by a round of laughter and congratulations. The atmosphere recovered and lighthearted. I smile at the surrounding scene. How could I have ever questioned their loyalty? Their support. Their love.

Cal pulls me to the side and explains Cyn hasn't been doing too well and has retreated to her bed.

Apparently, a doctor has been over at the house to sedate her. Lily is there with Chloe and Reece while Jack has been looking after Keen.

The guys say their goodbyes. The love obvious as they each hug their brother, then me.

I'm just about to relax when the door swings open, making both me and Con jump retrospectively. I turn sharply to find a disheveled-looking Brennan standing in the doorway. Instinctively, my body goes into defense and protection mode. I march in front of Con's bed with my arms crossed before me ready for battle.

There's no way in hell Con will be a victim to Brennan's demeaning, vicious, unsympathetic tongue. No way in hell.

Brennan eyes me cautiously. His usual broad shoulders slackened. The darkness under his eyes clear of a man who has been through hell. Sympathy oozes into my heart. His normally vibrant, deep-blue eyes now completely drained and remorseful.

He sighs, then shuffles on the spot, clearly out of his comfort zone. "Ya gonna let me in, lass? Ain't gonna hurt him." His sharp eyes meet mine.

"Will, let Da through the door," Con gently speaks from behind.

I lower my shoulders and move to the side, giving way for Brennan to barge past me. My nostrils flare, and I deep breathe to rein in my temper before spinning on my heels to give him a piece of my mind.

The scene before me is truly heartbreaking and all my aggression is instantly dismissed. Brennan is holding a sobbing Con in his arms in an enormous bear hug.

I stifle my own sob with a hand to my mouth,

desperate to not interrupt the rare show of love and support.

Brennan whispers words to Con, and Con holds Brennan tighter, his fists clutching at Brennan's suit jacket. A loving moment between father and son. I feel privileged to have witnessed a glimmer.

Once again, this is a reminder of the relationship that Con has with Keen. It's unlike anything he's ever received himself. He gives himself whole-heartedly to Keen, a stark contrast from his own relationship with his father. He's determined to be a better man.

Brennan pulls away, and Con nods at him. Then he straightens his shoulders back, tugs his jacket at the bottom to pull it into place, raises his chin in the air and reverts to his normal arrogant ass self almost in an instant. The change in air a witness to the transformation.

His deep voice bounces off the walls. "Now, pull a stunt like that again, ya little shite, and I'll kill you myself, ya hear me?" My eyes bug out at his crude words.

Con's lips curl up at the corner, almost in a laugh. His playful eyes meet mine, and I know he hasn't taken his father's words to heart. Thank God.

Brennan stands towering above Con's bed waiting for a response. "Yeah, Da. I hear ya." Brennan nods in approval, spins, and walks out the door. My mouth hangs open in shock at the turn of events.

We both sigh a breath of relief as the door closes.

Con's eyes dance knowingly at my reaction.

"I'm going to go and check on Keen. Will you be okay for a little while?"

"As long as you come back." Con's eyes suddenly become vulnerable.

I go over to his bed and climb in. Gently, I tuck his head into my chest and kiss the top of his wavy hair, cradling him. Con's body sags into mine at the ease of my affection. "I'll always come back for you."

"Me too. I love you always."

Chapter Thirty-Three

Con

It's been just over eight weeks since Keen's birthday, and a lot has fucking changed in that time.

With the help of Oscar, he got me an awesome doctor who diagnosed me with PTSD, anxiety, and depression, I'm on a few different drugs that have helped stabilize my mood. I also see a therapist twice a week. A little extreme if you ask me, but I do what Will wants. For us.

Not going to lie, it's fucking hard work going over how I feel each session. But this last week, it definitely seems to be getting easier, lighter.

Will and I couldn't be any stronger. She's my everything, and I'm finally certain I'm hers too. Keen made a full recovery. Being the little warrior he is, he bounced back like a fucking superstar.

We moved into our new home last month, and it's quickly becoming my sanctuary. I can't wait to get back to my family every day. And even when our puppy shits everywhere, I wouldn't want to be anywhere else. It's home.

———

I pull the car to a stop in the driveway of our parents' house and recognize I don't feel the same anxiety I used to. I couldn't pinpoint when it started, but I know when it ended. When my da hugged me for the first time in my life. He loves me and wants me, Connor O'Connell, to be with him. His family.

"You, okay?" Will asks me for the hundredth fucking time. I turn to her, and she bites her bottom lip, realizing she's asked again. Her beautiful hazel eyes meet mine in apology. I stroke my hand down her face and lean in and gently kiss those perfect lips. The lips that woke me this morning wrapped around my cock; the memory makes my cock twitch. She sighs easily into the kiss.

I pull back and lock eyes with hers. "I'm fine, baby." Brushing my mouth against her ear, I softly whisper, with grit in my tone, "You ask me one more time, Will, and I'm gonna spank that ass raw." She shudders and goose bumps break out over her arms. My girl loves my filthy mouth.

"Daddy, can we get out now?" Keen whines, breaking the tension. I draw away from Will and adjust myself through my jeans, pulling my T-shirt out over the top of my raging cock. The little minx grins at me.

———

The family is gathered around the table as Ma proudly lays out the food. We've brought along Peppa, our family puppy, as Keen insisted. He's sitting daintily on the table next to Puss. Both of them eating from Reece's hands. Cute as fuck.

"So, the dog is a male, but you called it fucking Peppa?" Finn quizzes, his eyes oozing disgust while pointing his toothpick at our puppy. My lazy, relaxed vibe I was rocking a second ago obliterated at his snide comment.

I straighten my shoulders and shrug. "It was either that or Cock. But we persuaded Keen to call him Peppa." I was quite proud I turned that one around.

Bren chokes on his meal. "You dodged a fucking bullet there."

I sit prouder. "Yeah. I suggested Peppa." My proud smile grows wider when Will beams up at me.

"Well, I like Cock!" Keen announces, making me sit forward in my seat.

"Keen, buddy. We agreed on Peppa. He makes little snorty noises just like the Peppa on television." I nod at Keen encouragingly.

"Well, I think Cock suits him better. And Cock loves Pussy." Finn's voice is laced in glee, his eyes locked onto the scene on the table. "I mean, see ... Pussy is licking Cock." He points at my dog.

Puss is showing him some love. Cute as fuck, but I turn my eyes on Finn and make sure he knows I'm pissed at him. My voice low and deadly. "It's Peppa," I seethe the words through clenched teeth.

Finn scoffs in jest. "You sappy shit. You've completely lost your balls to a kid and a dog. Hell, the dog has bigger balls than you."

I glare venomously at him. "Shut the fuck up. Peppa's cute as shit; it suits him."

My da chokes. His voice bellows through the room. "Fecking cute? Finn's right, you've lost your feckin' balls. Bet the feckin' thing ate 'em."

Cal turns his head from side to side, scrutinizing Peppa. I wish like fuck they'd all leave him alone. He's the bomb. "The dog looks like he's had a severe case of mange."

Finn chimes in. "I mean, what the fuck is it meant to be?"

My words come out pissed, with a threatening bite to them. Because let's face it, they're being dicks. "He's a Chinese Crested."

"He's a feckin' abomination. Looks like a feckin' rat. Get it off my table," Da shouts while pointing at Peppa.

Reece's eyes shoot up and blaze with poison.

He pushes his chair back and leaves the table.

We all watch him walk away. Our mouths open and eyes wide. That's not like Reece. Not at all.

Lily clears her throat to explain. "We've been working on him walking away from conflict, encouraging him to rein in his words." Her smile is proud and graceful.

The table begins congratulating them, and words of appraisal are shared. They do amazing with Reece, and the transformation in him is undeniable.

"What stage is Chloe at now?" Oscar asks. He's been monitoring Chloe's progress from a distance. Never getting too close. But his concern is touching. He hasn't said it, but it doesn't take a mastermind to figure out he's looking out for Chloe's development. To see if we have another genius in the family, no doubt.

Cal seems to miss the point completely. "She's at the teething stage. She's obsessed with Puss too." We all smile at little Chloe as she mushes up her food in the palms of her chubby hands.

Reece slumps back in his chair, drawing attention away from Chloe. His face is sulky and petulant.

Will

We all laugh and chat around the table. The atmosphere soothing, the warmth and love of the family encircling my heart.

Cyn hands out the desserts. She's made a yummy apple pie, and Brennan has his usual bread and butter pudding. The man is religious in his meals.

All too soon, the mood changes. Brennan coughs, thumping his fist against his chest and gasping for breath.

"Da, are you okay?" Cal panics, getting up from the table. Da waves him away, hating appearing weak. Heaven forbid.

"Pass him the water," Ma suggests. Cal does as Cyn instructs, and Brennan swallows a full glass worth.

His cough settles down but occasionally reappears, making him bristle with annoyance. Silently irritating him as he tries to ignore it and continues on eating his dessert. We all eye each other with uncertainty if he's okay but not wanting to make a show of the situation.

He gasps a deep breath and chokes heavily.

Yeah. He's not okay. What the hell?

"Da. What's wrong?" Bren snaps, impatient as ever. Like father, like son and all that.

Finn sits back lazily in his chair, watching the drama unfold.

"Can you speak?" Cal stupidly asks. The man's face is red, and he's clutching his throat.

"I'll call 911." Oscar sighs, drawing his words out nonchalantly, as if he couldn't care less to ring 911.

Lily shoots out of her chair. "Oh, my gosh. Is he having a heart attack?" Panic floods the room as everyone rises slowly from their seats to assist in one way or another.

Reece jumps up, his chair hitting the floor with an echoing clatter. All eyes on him. "Jesus. He's fine. Calm the fuck down. It's just a bit of pepper." He shrugs, takes his seat again, and continues eating his dessert.

Lily's eyes flare.

Cal can't get his words out. "P ... pepper?"

Reece slowly tilts his head to face Cal. "Yeah. Pepper. Not a fucking heart attack." He rolls his eyes with boredom.

"Pepper?" Cal questions again.

I look at Finn, his grin encompassing his mouth.

"Fucking pepper?" Cal rages, his voice high. Lily strokes his arm, trying to soothe him.

"Ya son feckin' poisoned me! The little bastard nearly killed me!" Da spits.

"Well, perhaps you shouldn't be so mean to Peppa. Besides, if I wanted to kill you, I'd use Botulinum." Reece shrugs.

Lily's mouth drops open, gaping like a fish. Open,

shut. Open, shut. Her feet slightly stumble at Reece's admission.

Cal and Lily spend the rest of the meal trying to chastise Reece, who scowls at their every word. Obviously, in complete disagreement with them.

I think Lily and Cal need to teach Reece to not use actions when he walks away from conflict as well as words, but I decide to keep that suggestion to myself.

Brennan retreated to his room, sulking. Cyn sits at the table proudly, smiling and shaking her head at all the drama.

I lean back in my chair, Con's arm draped over my back. I turn my head to him, my voice delicate. "You okay?" Con's nostrils flare, he raises an eyebrow, and I bite my lip in response to the deep black of his pupils expanding. My blood pumps around me, my panties becoming uncomfortable.

Con pulls my lip from between my teeth with his thumb. "You won't be able to sit down for a week." His dark voice makes me shudder.

Jesus, he's hot.

"Keen, come on, buddy. Time to go home." My eyes dance playfully at Con, a smug grin spreading across his face.

Bring it on.

Bring it fucking on.

Epilogue

Con

"Face down, ass up, baby," I demand.

"Is that really necessary?" Will snarks back.

I nod at the bed. "Absolutely. You know it pisses me off when you keep asking me if I'm okay. Now be a good girl and take your punishment." I smirk at my words.

Will drops her head slightly. "I just care."

I lift her chin with my fingers. "I know, baby, and I appreciate it. Now, stop with the excuses and get on the fucking bed. Ass high."

She does as I tell her. And Jesus fucking Christ, she's hot. So hot I could blow my fucking load just looking at her pert ass in the air.

We're both naked, locked in our bedroom. Keen and Peppa safely tucked up. Now it's time for Will to receive her punishment.

I stroke her ass cheek, tingles breaking out over my body at the touch. Will shudders, clearly just as affected.

I raise my right hand. *Smack!* Straight on that perky ass. Her body jolts into the mattress. Fuck yeah. I lick my lips.

I stroke it, soothing it gently before raising my palm and repeating the action. "Fuck, Con."

Smack! "You sorry, baby?"

Smack! I soothe her once again.

"Fuck yes. I'm sorry," she pants out. Her little moans are igniting my need to fill her. To drown her in my cum.

"Are you going to do it again?" *Smack!*

Will struggles to catch her breath. I watch her as she bites into her lip before answering, "Honestly? Probably."

Her answer makes me chuckle. Yeah, she'll definitely do it again. I lean over her body, to her ear. Gently, I stroke her hair, pushing it behind her ear. "Guess I'm going to have to come up with a better punishment then, hey?!" She sucks in a breath, arousal filling my veins. I straighten up and move a hand to my cock, pumping it a few times before finding her dripping pussy. I surge forward, knocking the wind out of her.

I stilt my actions, willing myself not to come. I always have the urge to come too soon with Will. I can never get enough. Never. The desperation to own her consumes me.

I gaze down at her body bent into the perfect curve and stroke over her spine. Up and down, all the way to her ass. As I surge forward again, I push my thumb into her ass. Will's mouth gapes open, "Oh, Jesus." I pound into her. "Oh god. Con." Her fists tighten in the sheets.

Fuck yeah. Her tight, wet pussy clenches around me. I pound and pound my hips against her tight little ass, the slapping noises of our skin filling the room. Fuck, she's hot.

I smack her ass again, and her firm walls hold my cock tighter and tighter, then they begin pulsating around me, the feeling rippling through me. Will tremors before screaming my name. "Co … nnn." The sensation spirals my own orgasm, her walls pulling it from me. I close my eyes and throw back my head at the ecstasy of my orgasm, the pulse of my cock flooding her pussy with my cum. I drop my mouth open in awe. Fuck, that's incredible.

I collapse beside Will and pull her into my arms. My chest still heaving. She raises her head, sweaty and sticky from our lovemaking. I rest on an elbow and stare down at my girl. Absolutely fucking beautiful.

"Marry me?" Her words come out so quickly I'm not sure I heard her right.

The confusion on my face makes her giggle. "Marry me, Con." Her eyes implore me, "Please?"

Jesus, I can't speak. I'm utterly fucking speechless. I stare into her beautiful hazel eyes, my lips parted to talk but unable to commit to the action. My eyes flare with hope. Did I hear her right?

"Can you speak?" she asks playfully, and I shake my head. No, I can't fucking speak.

I can't fucking function right now.

"Nod your head for yes. Shake it for no," Will says while chewing her lip.

I nod my head frenziedly.

Will chuckles and leans forward for a kiss. I flip us over and pounce on her mouth, my tongue finding hers with vigor. Sliding home into her pussy, my body comes alive once again. Will wraps her arms around my neck as I make love to her.

"I love you so damn much, baby," I tell her.

"I know. And I love you too, always." She smiles into our kiss, and I know right here and now, in one another's arms, we finally have our forever.

THE END

More?

Want a little more?

Would you like more of Con and Will?

Come and sign up to BJ Alpha's newsletter for an exclusive extra scene and be the first to hear about the up and coming events and book news.

Use the link to get your copy of Con & Will's extended epilogue now: **Extended Epilogue**

Also by B J Alpha

MAFIA DADDIES

Daddy's Addiction

POSSESSION

DECEPTION

DOMINATION

SECRETS AND LIES SERIES

CAL Book 1

CON Book 2

FINN Book 3

BREN Book 4

OSCAR Book 5

THE FINAL VOW

O'CONNELL'S FOREVER

BORN SERIES

BORN RECKLESS

THE BRUTAL DUET

HIDDEN IN BRUTAL DEVOTION

LOVE IN BRUTAL DEVOTION

THE BRUTAL DUET PART TWO

BRUTAL SECRETS

BRUTAL LIES

STORM ENTERPRISES

SHAW Book 1

TATE Book 2

OWEN Book 3

REED Book 4

VEILED IN SERIES

VEILED IN HATE

CARRERA FAMILY

STONE Book 1

AZRAEL Book 2

Acknowledgments

To my fellow Cygnets, thank you!
My soul sister, Jaclyn for always encouraging me and believing in me. You're one in a million Jaclyn.

Thank you to my Beta Readers, Libby, Rhi, Jaclyn, J and Em. I'm so thankful for your help and constant support.

An extra special thank you to Libby for absolutely everything, I'm in awe of your kindness. The fact that you go above and beyond for me is incredible.

A special mention to the Swan Squad.
This group of ladies lift me up and make me smile when I need it the most.
I've formed friendships through this amazing group of ladies that mean the world to me.
Emma H, Patricia B, Claire B, Caroline W and the amazing Bren with her swan cnuts. Thank you for your friendship and support.

My beautiful friends.
The crazy Kate. Your journey is only just beginning, and I cannot wait to see where it takes you! Preferably with me attached to you. Or the other way round, whatever.

Marie N thank you for EVERY. THING! Thank you for
being you.
To my friends Julie and Hayden, thank you for being my
biggest supporters. A reminder that family aren't always
blood.

Sarah and Meg, your words and photos lift me up. Keep
going girl, super proud of you. Thank you for always
being a message away. x

To my ARC readers and bloggers. Thank you for all
your hard work, messages and support!

To my mum, thank you for your support.
Love you more.

To my boys, thank you for everything. I'm so incredibly
proud of you both, keep being you.

To my hubby, the J in my BJ. Thank you for pushing me,
listening to me and supporting me through this whole
process, yet again. Without you I wouldn't be BJ Alpha.
Love you trillions!

Thank you to https://www.mind.org.uk for the information available.
I'd also like to thank https://autism.org.uk for the
wealth of information available to me and many others.

And last but by no means least thank you to all my readers. I really hope you enjoyed Con as much as I did!

About the Author

BJ Alpha lives in the UK with her hubby, two teenage sons and three fur babies.
I love to both read and write hot alpha men and feisty females.

Join me on my social media pages…

For all news on upcoming books, visit my Facebook pages:
BJ Alpha Facebook Page

My readers group:
BJ's Reckless Readers

Instagram: BJ Alpha Instagram